PENGUIN BOOKS

YOU'RE NOT TOO OLD
TO HAVE A BABY

Jane Price was born in Long Beach, California, in 1944. She received her M.A. from
Harvard University and her Ph.D. in East
Asian history from Columbia University,
where she now teaches. Ms. Price waited to
have her first child until she was nearly
thirty-two. Her skills as a scholar and her
personal interest in delayed parenthood combine to make this book both authoritative
and sympathetic.

You're Not Too Old to Have a Baby

Jane Price

PENGUIN BOOKS

Penguin Books Ltd, Harmondsworth,
Middlesex, England
Penguin Books, 625 Madison Avenue,
New York, New York 10022, U.S.A.
Penguin Books Australia Ltd, Ringwood,
Victoria, Australia
Penguin Books Canada Limited, 2801 John Street,
Markham, Ontario, Canada L3R 1B4
Penguin Books (N.Z.) Ltd, 182–190 Wairau Road,
Auckland 10, New Zealand

First published in the United States of America by
Farrar, Straus and Giroux, Inc., 1977
First published in Canada by McGraw-Hill Ryerson Limited 1977
Published in Penguin Books 1978

LIBRARY OF CONGRESS CATALOGING IN PUBLICATION DATA
Price, Jane, 1944–
You're not too old to have a baby.
Reprint of the 1977 ed. published by Farrar, Straus,
Giroux, New York.
Bibliography: p. 145.
1. Pregnancy in middle age. 2. Childbirth in middle
age. 3. Parent and child. I. Title.
[RG556.6.P75 1978]   612.6′3   78-9876
ISBN 0 14 00.4910 X

Printed in the United States of America by
Offset Paperback Mfrs., Inc., Dallas, Pennsylvania
Set in Janson

To Ken and Erica

Contents

Introduction

"How long can you wait to have children?" This has become a common question among couples who see parenthood as a matter of choice. More and more women are seeking fulfillment in jobs or interests outside the home. They and their husbands want children very much, but they wonder about the impact on their lifestyle and the quality of their relationship.

How can children be reconciled with the needs of their parents? One strategy that is gaining popularity is to delay childbearing until later in life. On the horizon is a trend toward late parenthood, prolonging the birth of one's first child until one's thirties or forties.

My husband and I were among those who decided to wait. When we married seven years ago, we were unsure about having children at all. We were preoccupied with graduate degrees and teaching and wanted time to find out about ourselves.

But while the question of children was still open, we began to look closely at the parents we knew. We were intrigued by the couples who had their first child later. Many were very busy people, with both husband and wife in demanding jobs. Yet they spoke of their children as their greatest source of joy and relished every moment they spent with them. Some of these late parents were approaching middle age but they seemed very young at heart and handled the responsibilities of parents with enthusiasm and ease.

We liked what we saw so much that we decided to become parents, too. And we became convinced that waiting until our thirties—for us—was the only way to go. Had not an unusually convenient time to have a child arisen when it did (a break between teaching jobs gave me time for a self-made maternity leave), we probably would have waited longer.

Did we make the right decision? For us, yes. Before that time we truly weren't ready for a child, emotionally or financially. But deciding to wait to have children wasn't that easy. We had heard there were increased medical risks in having a child past the age of thirty. And we ran up against plenty of old wives' tales about being "too old" to have children psychologically. In fact, we found the currents of prejudice against older parents in this society remarkably strong.

Before having our child we began gathering information to help us make an intelligent decision. We wanted to get beyond the rumors and half truths to the real facts. Exactly how great are the medical risks in late childbearing? Could one be too old to be a good parent? What difference does age make in planning and raising a family? This book is an outgrowth of what began as a personal quest for answers to these questions.

What I found out about late parenthood for our own benefit was encouraging. But I decided to pursue the matter further for the sake of other couples as well. I'm convinced that many couples are pressured into having children too early because they lack adequate information on the alternatives. Having children later in life has many advantages and prospective parents should know what they are.

I've tried to look at delayed parenthood from every angle, surveying the medical, psychological, and social issues raised by having children later in life. I spent several months in medical libraries and talked to some of the leading authorities on problem pregnancies and late childbearing. I combed New York's libraries for the most recent family studies and met with specialists who treated family problems. I interviewed in depth over two dozen couples who had their first child in their thirties or forties. And I spoke with children of older parents and couples who had started families anew after their first set of children had grown up.

We have entered an era of profound change in the position of women. More are working than ever before and are searching for avenues of fulfillment beyond the motherhood role. This is one of the main reasons why couples are delaying parenthood. A big plus to waiting to have children is that it helps women combine career and family. And it gives women who are less job-oriented a chance to explore their identities. As more couples delay parenthood, they will have a decisive impact on our institutions and values. Some see the outcome of a movement toward late childbearing as controversial. I have tried to objectively explore the value of late parenthood and to clarify its relationship to broader changes in our society.

Medically, the risks of waiting to have children past the biological prime have been exaggerated. With recent advances in genetics and obstetrics, most mothers over thirty, thirty-five, and forty have an excellent chance of bearing a healthy child. A large part of this book looks into the childbearing problems associated with advancing age and what can be done about them.

I've found much to recommend older couples as good parents, too. There are a few problems characteristic of older parents and their families but there are also many areas where latecomers do very well. An entire chapter deals with the strengths and weaknesses of older parents and what they might anticipate as their children grow up.

Should everyone delay parenthood? Not necessarily, but I believe that everyone should know the entire range of issues that deciding when to have a child involves. If to wait or not to wait is the question, this book may help with the answer.

I am indebted to each of the couples I interviewed for their generosity and candor. Their names have been changed but I've kept their words and observations intact. My special thanks to Dr. Sheldon H. Cherry, Dr. Desider Rothe, Dr. Theodore Tobias, Dr. P. Theodore Watson, Dr. Shirley Van Ferney, Dr. Deborah Price, Professor Zonia Krassner, Professor Cynthia Fuchs Epstein, Ms. Sharon Yellin Glick, Ms. Frieda Nelson, and Ms. Kathryn Tener Smith for their expert advice, and to the staffs of the Planned Parenthood Library and New York Hospital–Cornell University Medical College library. This book could not have been completed without the timely suggestions and encouragement of my editor, Pat Strachan, and my colleague, Susan Previant Lee.

You're Not
Too Old to
Have a Baby

1

Who Waits to Have Children? And Why?

The cover of a 1976 issue of *Ms.* magazine featured a woman close to nine months pregnant. Her hair was flecked with gray and her eyes framed by wrinkles. She clearly was not one of the "young mamas" cultivated by women's magazines and television commercials. In some circles, minus her distended belly, she could have been taken for a grandmother.

This picture of an expectant mother nearly forty years old highlighted the magazine's lead article, "Over 30? Over 35? Over 40? How Late Can You Wait to Have a Baby?" While the cover and story were intended to capture readers' attention, they also confirmed an established social fact: more and more women in this country are delaying childbirth until they are well into their thirties. And "How late can you wait to have a baby?" is a question that growing numbers seriously ask.

Recent statistics are documenting a trend toward older parenthood. Demographers in California have reported a surging birth rate for women twenty-five to thirty-four between 1966 and 1974. Many of these women are first-time mothers who put off having children until their thirties. In 1974 almost one third of all married women under thirty had not had children, compared to one fourth in 1970 and one fifth in 1960. "It is not likely that such large proportions of married women will remain childless," say demographers June Sklar and Beth Berkov. "Among childless married women age 30 in 1974, more than three-fourths expected to have two or more children by the end of their childbearing period."

What is happening in California is being reflected nationwide: products of the postwar baby boom who decide to become older parents are creating a mini baby boom of their own. The National Center for Health Statistics reported a 6 percent rise in first births during 1974 for women twenty-five to thirty-nine at a time when first births on the average were increasing by only 1 percent and the national birth rate continued to decline.

All indicators point to the fact that couples are marrying and starting their families later. Reversing a century-long trend, the age at which women marry and have children has risen since 1965. That year the median age for a woman bearing her first child was 21.9; by 1971 it had climbed to 22.1. While this rise isn't dramatic, it does reflect the beginning of a movement toward delaying childbearing in a society where one third of the women give birth to their first child by the time they're twenty years old.

Part of this trend can be attributed to young brides who put off having children for several years but still start their families in their twenties. But the number of women who don't have children until their thirties or forties continues to mount. In some areas the visibility of older parents is quite striking.

"I've seen a definite increase in patients over thirty

having their first child during the past five years," says Dr. Sheldon H. Cherry, obstetrician-gynecologist at Mount Sinai Hospital in New York and assistant clinical professor of obstetrics and gynecology at the Mount Sinai School of Medicine. Manhattan obstetrician Theodore Tobias, who is also associated with Mount Sinai, has observed that the average age of his first-time maternity patient is now about thirty.

It's common to find couples in their thirties and early forties preparing for their first births in childbirth classes at Mount Sinai and New York Hospital. And the growing numbers of older mothers are beginning to revolutionize maternity fashions, too. Mater's Market, a Manhattan maternity boutique, is putting out designs for older women. "I noticed that women were becoming pregnant at an older age and had more money to spend, but they were having a difficult time finding elegant things to wear to business dinners and such," said co-owner Myrna Tarnower.

This movement toward delayed parenthood is, however, a minority trend—only about 5 percent of women having their first child in 1974 were thirty or over. But the trend will grow more pronounced in middle- and upper-income groups, especially in our large urban centers.

Dr. P. Theodore Watson, a prominent obstetrician-gynecologist in St. Paul-Minneapolis, has observed that his patients now produce their first children five years later than they used to. "Most of them marry when they are between twenty and twenty-four and deliver before they are thirty," he told me. "But they are still older than they were before." If New York and California are in the vanguard, one will see the number of older parents multiply in other American cities as well in the next few years. Perhaps five years from now the average age of Dr. Watson's first-time maternity patients will be over thirty. First-time mothers in their late thirties will never become a majority, but they are no longer an anomaly.

Why Some People Wait

What accounts for the rise in first-time mothers over thirty and the trend toward older parenthood? First of all, more Americans are delaying the age at which they marry. While most men and women still wed young, the average marriage age has climbed slowly since 1960. There are sufficient numbers of young people—especially women—delaying entry into matrimony to raise the average age of first marriages by one month every year. Over the past decade the median marriage age of American women has thus risen from twenty to twenty-one years.

Those who come late to married life may reflect the impersonal forces of demography. Some single women now in their thirties are products of the "marriage squeeze," an oversupply of marriageable women relative to the number of eligible males. Since women in this country tend to marry men older than themselves, those born while World War II was underway most often found their supply of mates from the males born during the lean childbearing years of the thirties. Although some victims of the "marriage squeeze" eventually find spouses from among younger males or formerly married men, many marry and start their families later.

Women are also remaining single longer out of conscious choice. The proliferation of apartment houses, bars, and consumer items geared to young unmarrieds testifies to the growing popularity of the solitary lifestyle. Women, as well as men, find the pursuit of a career and the freedom of living alone an attractive option. The number of marriages in the United States fell by nearly 3 percent in the year ending August 1974. Our country is now witnessing the first significant decline in its marriage rate since World War II, and as marriages are postponed, births are, too.

In a larger sense, the decision to forgo or postpone having children is an outgrowth of the transformation in the institution of marriage. In more traditional societies, such as our country one hundred years ago, marriage had several key functions: it provided a setting for procreation and an anchor for one's ties to community and job. Old-style marriages had clearly prescribed roles for husbands and wives: a good wife had many children and took care of the home; a good husband was the family provider. Marriage was synonymous with having children—one wed to "start a family." Love and emotional attachment were relegated to the background.

The permanent contractual relationship between husband and wife still carries certain financial advantages and is still associated with the rearing of children. However, most people today see marriage primarily as an interpersonal relationship that satisfies certain emotional needs. Children are no longer the economic asset they were when most families lived on farms or ran small businesses. Their labor cannot easily be translated into family income and they aren't as likely to support their parents in old age.

Reproduction has ceased to be an economic necessity and children have become a luxury option. "Children have . . . been viewed as consumer goods," states sociologist Jessie Bernard, one of this country's leading authorities on the family. "The young husband and working wife ask themselves when they can 'afford' to have children and how many they can 'afford.'"

Industrialization has speeded the transformation of family life, opening up a new range of jobs for women. They are now able to choose occupations other than wife and mother and have been given additional impetus from the women's liberation movement to change their traditional roles. "As recently as ten years ago, a woman had to defend her position if she wanted to work," observed Beatrice Buckler, former editor of *Working Woman* magazine. "Now you have only to go out and ask the nearest housewife what she does and she'll answer, 'I'm just a housewife.' There's been a tremendous change in attitude."

The number of women who work outside the home has been rising since 1947, but the most striking changes in their status have occurred since the mid-sixties. Record numbers of women of all ages have surged into the labor force. By 1976, 38.6 million women, constituting two fifths of the entire labor force, were working or seeking work. This move outside the home reflects both the expansion of job opportunities for women and changes in women's conception of themselves. Columbia University economist Eli Ginzburg, chairman of the National Commission for Manpower Policy, calls this trend "the single most outstanding phenomenon of our century."

Today, two fifths of all married women are in the labor force, compared to one fourth in the mid-fifties. Forty-eight percent of American women sixteen and older are working women, in contrast to 23 percent in 1920. And the fastest rate of entrance into the work force has come from women between the ages of twenty and thirty-four.

The nature of jobs open to women has affected their attitudes toward work outside the home. While much of the expansion has been in traditionally "female" jobs—clerical work, waitressing, secretarial work, nursing, etc.—women have also been gaining access to high-level employment. Increased educational opportunities have enabled them to compete for interesting and lucrative positions. The number of women in professional and technical jobs is on the rise. In 1970 the Department of

Labor classified 4.3 million women, 15 percent of the female labor force, as "professional and technical workers," compared to 2.7 million, or 13 percent of the female labor force, ten years earlier.

Women with a relatively high level of education and income are more likely to stick with their jobs than those who are ill-educated and poorly paid. They tend to delay marriage and childbearing much longer and generally wind up with smaller families. It is this privileged group that has supplied most of the older parents on the current scene. The greatest increase in labor-force participation among college graduates has come from women between twenty-five and thirty-four, the period when most would normally leave work to raise children.

Attractive jobs now require more years of training than they did twenty years ago. For both men and women, job-related educational requirements have put a brake on marriage and childbearing. Young people are reluctant to start families when costly training lies ahead of them. Many of those who complete their education want to enjoy the fruit of their careers before taking on the burden of additional dependents. As one M.A. candidate at the City University of New York put it, "Now I have a good job that pays $18,000 a year, a luxury apartment, a Porsche, and a fabulous stereo system and jazz collection. I'm not ready to get married and have children; why should I give all this up? If I do get married—which won't be for a long time—I'll expect my wife to work, too."

If young adults wish to postpone marriage or childbearing, recent advances in birth control have made that choice possible. Contraception in this country is not new, but genuinely effective forms of birth control have been available for only the past fifteen years. Before the Pill and the IUD most people obtained their contraceptives from the local drugstore. The diaphragm, which has been available to women through physicians since the turn of the century, is nearly foolproof if properly used, but it doesn't allow for spontaneous sex. Before the sixties successful practitioners of birth control were those who either resisted the sweep of passion or had a high degree of luck.

Today, those who use the Pill, an IUD, or abortion as a last resort need leave little to chance. Birth control is no longer a gamble, and people can, for the first time, actually control their fertility. While these developments have cut down illegitimacy and unwanted pregnancy among the poor, the chief beneficiaries have been members of the middle class, who, by virtue of their education and commitment to careers, are more likely to follow through on birth control correctly and conscientiously.

Inexpensive abortion on demand has been particularly useful to young couples seeking to delay parenthood. Before its legalization, most women seeking abortion were unmarried. Now many patients of abortion clinics are married women who wish to limit their families or postpone child rearing. It has been estimated that one third of the 900,000 legal abortions performed in 1974 were on women who would have completed their pregnancies if legal termination were not an option. A decade earlier, abortions were expensive, illegal, and frequently dangerous; women who did not fear illegitimacy shied away from the risk and expense.

Economics now figure heavily in a couple's timing of childbearing, and improved methods of birth control, as well as legalized abortion, have lent more control to this conscious scheduling. People have children for a wide range of motives: they may believe reproduction a social or religious obligation; they may find children a source of novelty and stimulation; they may need children to bolster their sense of accomplishment or to confirm their sexual identity. Some couples with a weak interpersonal relationship find children their only source of marital happiness. But few parents in this country today expect to come out ahead financially.

Most couples cite finances as the primary reason for restricting family size: "We want to provide a better quality of life for our children and ourselves." And recent recessionary turns in the American economy have made having children even more financially burdensome. In 1975 the average number of children born to each family plummeted to 1.8, less than half of what it was in 1957. For the vast majority of Americans, a family of two children has become "ideal."

Some credit for the growing popularity of the small family should go to the environmental movement. Until very recently there was enormous cultural and social pressure to marry and have children. Couples who did not have offspring were often labeled "selfish" or "weird," and most families were encouraged to have as many children as they could afford. Our developing knowledge of the social and environmental problems linked to population pressures has become a counterforce to the pronatalists. We now have active organizations promoting a "zero population growth," the voluntary limitation of two children to a couple, and even a National Organization for Non-Parents. It has become increasingly common for couples to swear off reproduction. In some circles, having children meets with the same critical reception formerly reserved for the childless. It is doubtful that people who forgo or limit childbearing do so for the sake of the environment alone. But antinatalist sentiment can bolster other, more personal, reasons for starting a family later and limiting its size.

The large-scale changes in our society that have altered our conceptions of family and parenthood have also found expression in new conjugal styles. While larger numbers of Americans are remaining single, they are not necessarily living alone. Couples are living together as a form of single lifestyle or as an alternative to marriage. Some mutual living arrangements become "trial marriages," which eventually turn into the real thing. But whatever the reason, living together out of wedlock usually involves a moratorium on having children. Many who become older parents have experimented with this type of arrangement for a number of years before signing an official marriage contract.

Divorce, which has reached epidemic proportions, can also encourage older parenthood. Thirty-seven percent of all first marriages in this country end in divorce and one million people now file into the nation's divorce courts every year. Four out of five remarry, usually to another divorced person. Recoupling generally takes place about three years after the divorce, and the average age for second marriages is around thirty for women and thirty-five for men. Those with childless first marriages don't have another opportunity for childbearing until they reach their thirties.

Do our rising rate of divorce and falling rate of marriage, a smaller family size and changing conception of family life foreshadow an end to marriage and parenthood? The answer is clearly no. We may be marrying and reproducing less and divorcing more, but the interest in marriage and children is as high as ever. A nationwide poll conducted in 1974 showed that only 1 percent of men and women in this country wish to remain single or live alone. Most young people are still in favor of having children, even those with attractive single lifestyles.

A series of studies has shown that the vast majority of career-oriented women see their jobs as adjuncts to husband and family. According to Joseph Veroff and Sheila Feld, authors of *Marriage and Work in America*, "Motherhood still remains a role in which an educated woman can find the personal gratification she needs to justify her existence." "Parenthood is an important stage and child rearing is an important function in the life of an adult," says psychiatrist Henry Greenbaum. "To downgrade them is to ignore deep human psychological needs."

This perhaps explains why many couples who have full lives without children eventually decide to have them. Writer Gail Sheehy, who studied stages of adult development, feels that women in their thirties become sensitive to needs left unfulfilled when they were younger. If they devoted themselves to their careers, they are likely to focus more on their personal lives.

Sheehy believes that when such women near the age of thirty-five, they may develop an intense desire for children. "Thirty-five brings the biological boundary into sight," she says. "Probably for the first time a woman glimpses that vague, uncharted realm ahead leading to what demographers so aridly call the end of her 'fecund and bearing years.'" Ms. Sheehy and others have theorized that the approach of menopause triggers an urge to assert the reproductive function before it is taken away. Psychoanalyst Helene Deutsch refers to this last-minute desire for children as "closing the gates."

In having a child late in life, couples also have the chance to participate in an experience usually reserved for the young. Ours is a society that glorifies youthfulness; combating the aging process is something of a national preoccupation. This youth mystique may operate as a subliminal catalyst for late parenthood. Observes a Manhattan prepared-childbirth instructor: "I've seen older couples react to the experience of having a child as if they're young again. Going through childbirth together takes away their age."

A number of older parents have told me that having a child as they neared middle age made them feel younger. "It keeps me young," said the fifty-year-old father of a fourth-grader. President Jimmy Carter reacted the same way to the birth of his daughter when he was in his forties. "She made me feel young again," he wrote. I'm not suggesting that older parents have children for the same reasons they go to exercise classes or use face cream, but having a baby later on does keep them in an earlier stage of the life cycle. In our society, the power of children to revitalize and refresh is part of the host of forces encouraging men and women to become parents much later than they did in the past.

Older Mothers: Who Are They?

What kinds of people delay parenthood? Some are luminaries such as Margaret Mead, Barbara Walters, newscasters Pat Collins on WCBS-TV, New York, and Pia Lindstrom on WNBC-TV, Congresswomen Yvonne Brathwaite Burke of California and Helen Stevenson Meyner of New Jersey. Many of the women I interviewed personally, though not of celebrity status, fell into the same category: they were exceptional achievers in business and the professions who had from early on pursued ambitious life goals.

But quite a few of the women I studied weren't high-flying career women. Some had left their jobs when they had children or had turned to other lines of work. However, they, like the career women, shared the sentiment expressed by one older mother: "I didn't have my baby because I wanted to be a mother but because I wanted a child." All of these women found great joy in motherhood. But they did not see themselves as mothers only and their lives were not entirely bound by their families.

A number of the women I spoke with explicitly decided to develop their careers before starting families. Ellen, now a vice-president in a metropolitan bank, didn't marry until her early thirties; she had her first child when she was thirty-three. She came from a family where the women were of exceptionally strong character, and had been educated at a top Ivy League university before starting out on Wall Street. "I knew I always wanted children," she said, "but there were other things that had to come first. For one, I wanted to wait until I became a bank officer before having children." She now has a son and daughter and attributes part of her success in combining career and family to her decision to wait.

"I don't think I was ready to marry when I was in my twenties," said Rachel, one of the most committed professional educators I've ever encountered. "I spent a year trying to get married before I met my husband, but gave up, realizing my career ought to come first. I became so frightened of the men I chose that I realized the reason I chose them was that I wasn't ready to get married." She met and married her husband, another teacher, when she was thirty-one.

Rachel believes her mother was a decisive influence on her aspirations. Her mother had been a promising concert pianist whose performances were reviewed in *The New York Times*. But she came from a Jewish working-class family where the sons' education came first, so she had to give up her musical career to support her brothers. In reaction to her own childhood, she encouraged her own daughter to go to college and graduate school.

Rachel waited until she was thirty-seven before having a child. "I thought of myself as a professional woman," she recalls. "But I still went through a period where something in me said, 'You're not someone unless you're married and have children.' I began to feel my age impinge on me when I was thirty-five and knew there was more of a problem with birth defects in women thirty-five and older. It was about that time I decided to become pregnant."

Rachel gave birth to her son when she accompanied her husband on a year-long research trip abroad. She went back to work as soon as she returned to this country and now teaches in one of the most highly regarded elementary schools in the New York City school system. She has a city-wide reputation as an articulate and innovative educator.

For Marian, the question was not one of reconciling childbearing to heavy career demands but whether she could fit children into a freewheeling lifestyle. She was well educated: a B.A. from Radcliffe and an M.A. from Columbia University in political science; one year in Japan on a Fulbright Fellowship. Marian left graduate school just short of her doctorate and held a number of jobs ranging from assistant director of examinations for the College Entrance Examination Board to secretarial work. She did not marry until she was thirty-one.

Neither Marian nor her husband associated getting married with having children, nor were they sure they ever wanted them. At the time of their wedding, Marian's husband, who was four years younger than she, had just begun law school. Under the circumstances, both put off the question of children to concentrate on other aspects of their relationship. They traveled to Europe seven times in seven years, and Marian was very pleased with her work and marriage. But she gradually became convinced that she wanted a child. "Six years after we were married," she told me, "I announced to my husband one day: 'I really would like to have a child.'" Her husband reacted negatively at first. He feared children would threaten their lifestyle and relationship, and didn't want his wife to give up work and outside activities. They agreed that a full-time housekeeper would ameliorate traumatic changes and decided to have a child.

Marian feels that their postponement of parenthood until she was thirty-nine may have been influenced by her and her husband's family background, as well as by lifestyle and career considerations. Both had parents who married late. Marian's mother had married when she was thirty-one and had her eldest daughter a year later. Her husband, an only child, was born to a woman of thirty-eight.

Marian found her pregnancy "a total delight from beginning to end." With the aid of her housekeeper, she returned to work a year after her daughter's birth. Her job, involving semi-administrative work at a major university, takes up only three days a week. She and her family divide their time between their New York City apartment and a country home. A measure of affluence has allowed Marian to strike a balance between several worlds—motherhood, work, recreation, and travel.

I found a number of women like Marian who had lives that were just too far-ranging for early motherhood. Hilary, accustomed to a highly independent life, had lived in Europe before coming to this country. She had taught at a West Coast university for five years. None of her relationships with men had resulted in marriage, but she decided to have a child when she was forty-one.

When she found out she had conceived, she was elated. "I thought I might be starting menopause, but I was actually pregnant," she said. "Perhaps this was my last chance to have a child." Hilary still works and may eventually marry, but, having spent most of her childhood in a one-parent family, she doesn't consider marriage necessary to parenthood.

The woman who came closest to seeing herself exclusively as a mother was Stephanie, an artist married to a social worker. She had come from a family where the women married young and where children came as naturally as eating and breathing. But she went to college at a leading midwestern university and on to a job in Chicago. She supported her artistic work by teaching for six years and didn't meet her husband until she was nearly thirty.

Had Stephanie remained in her home town, she might have married and had children sooner. But she had become part of a sophisticated urban circle where men and women waited to settle down. She married much later than other members of her family. Because of fertility problems, she bore her first child at thirty-four and her second at thirty-six. "I want to stay at home until they're older," she said. "I can do some painting there and take a couple of classes." Stephanie intends to resume her serious artistic work when her children are in school.

Statistically, older mothers like Ellen, Marian, and Hilary will always be a minority. But we can expect to see more women like them in the future. Who are the strongest candidates for older parenthood? Certainly older mothers cannot be confined to one occupational or personality type. But if one were to draw a composite profile, it might look like this: a college education or special training sufficient for a lucrative or interesting job; a well-developed set of tastes, interests, and activities outside the home; residence in or near a large urban area. This type of woman will not confine her friends to married couples with children. She may be married or single, but will not equate having children with "a woman's role." And she will not have married to "start a family."

The Case for Older Parenthood

Older parents are a growing social phenomenon. But is this trend good or bad? Should more people be encouraged to delay having children in the future? Can one make an actual case for older parenthood? Certainly from a financial point of view there are many advantages to postponing childbearing until one's thirties. A trained money manager or expert on family finances would probably nod vigorously with approval.

Daily living has become very costly and insecure, and there is little relief in sight for the future. An individual attempting to steer a course between inflation and unemployment will find supporting himself risky enough. The going is that much more rough if he has to provide for others as well.

Let's start with maternity costs. Babies aren't delivered by storks free of charge. The bill for the obstetrician, hospital room, delivery room, and nursery can run from mildly hefty to downright staggering figures. The most expensive place in the United States to have a baby is New York City. There, charges average about $2,000 per child. With complications, a private hospital room, or ultra-fancy obstetrician, the bill can run 50 percent higher. As one moves outside the New York metropolitan area, these expenses go down. The average cost of childbirth for most of the country is slightly less than half of that in the Big Apple. Still, that's a lot of cash to muster and most medical plans cover only a fraction of maternity expenses. One can mitigate the pinch to the pocketbook by using a maternity clinic, or—if one is a bit daring and in good health—by having the baby at home.

Aside from basics in food, clothing, and shelter, the cost of raising a child varies with parents' income level and tastes. But assuming one forgoes such popular "extras" as professional baby photographs and silver feeding spoons, the wallet will be lightened by about $1,500 during the infant's first year alone—for food, clothing, nursery furniture, diapers and laundry, visits to the pediatrician, and a few toys. That's a relatively conservative estimate for a middle-income family. Those who wish to maintain an active social life should add the cost of babysitters as well.

Child-rearing expenses climb as the child gets older: it costs 30 to 45 percent more to support an eighteen-year-old than a one-year-old—and that excludes college. *Esquire* magazine estimated in March 1974 that the price of one "good to superior-quality child" in a major city could run as high as $25,000 for the first five years; $55,000 for ages six through eleven; and $54,000 for ages twelve through seventeen. These amounts could be lowered about 50 percent by eliminating private school, braces, and summer camp. Nevertheless, that would still leave the average pre-college cost of each child a whopping $80,000. Then there's college: $5,000 to $7,000 a year for tuition, room, and board at most private institutions; about half that amount annually at state universities or publicly supported schools. The lucky few will be able to cut corners through scholarships or by having college-age children live at home.

An upper-middle-class urban family could thus run the cost of one child from conception through graduate or professional school to over $200,000. For most of us, this figure is high. But how much lower can we go? A recent study, "Costs of Children," by the Commission for Population Growth and the American Future, put the bill for raising two children, in a typical American family from birth through college, at between $80,000 and $150,000. In other words, the "direct cost" of rearing one child is still approximately 15 to 17 percent of family income.

What can push these figures toward the higher range is the "opportunity costs" of child rearing for women—the potential earnings a woman forfeits to stay at home with her family. Opportunity costs rise with the level of a woman's education and earning power. A mother who remains at home until her youngest child reaches fourteen will "lose" earnings totaling $58,904 if she completed high school, $82,467 if she had a college degree, and $103,023 if she had postgraduate training.

High opportunity costs help account for the large

proportion of educated women who limit their family size and remain in the work force. Children cost them more. Here the older woman has a distinct advantage. She is generally well established in her career and more likely to win from her employer time for a maternity leave or a flexible work schedule. Her salary may be high enough to afford child care. Seniority gives her a vested interest in continuing her job.

There are other forms of indirect cost that raise the bill for children even higher—increased rent on larger living quarters or the mortgage on a house; lawyer's fees to draw up a will; washing machine and dryer; a new life-insurance policy. Some of these expenses may be offset by tax deductions for additional dependents and high medical expenses (the first child is a bit more costly than the others), but under present conditions parenthood must be associated with heavy financial responsibilities.

In addition to dealing with the opportunity-cost factor for women, the older couple is in a much stronger position to meet child-related expenses all around. If one were able to save all the money needed to raise the child before its birth, it would be possible to reduce yearly child-rearing costs substantially. Interest would accrue on the original amount or portions of it while smaller amounts were being spent for the child on a yearly basis. Assuming an annual interest of 8 percent on the unspent portion of the money, the cost of raising a first child could be "discounted." The couple who has been working a number of years would be most capable of amassing the savings required.

It is also the case that salary levels for the older couple will generally be higher than those of their younger counterparts. Salaries for those aged thirty-five to forty-four tend to rise more rapidly than for those under thirty-four. Older parents should also prove more capable of managing what money they have. People now under thirty grew up during the most prosperous period in our nation's history, when their parents' incomes rose faster than prices for goods and services. They experienced gains in real income in the form of a rising standard of living—and rising expectations. Many in this generation anticipate the same level of material luxury they grew up with and are tempted to spend beyond their means when they set up their own households. The older couple has more time in which to learn how to budget—and how to do without—and are much more likely to anticipate and plan for the additional financial strains that children bring.

What Would Marriage Counselors Say?

Child rearing also places heavy strains on a couple's emotional resources. To be a parent is to take responsibility not only for oneself but for the lives of others. Biologically, many Americans could reproduce by the time they reach their teens. But the psychological preparation for parenthood takes much longer.

Most child rearing in this country takes place within the institution of marriage. And age has a positive effect on marital stability—partial assurance that a couple can create an appropriate setting to raise their young. It is more likely that an older couple has attained sufficient maturity to sustain a complex interpersonal relationship. A young person can have experiences that make him "old for his years," but most people need to ripen with age. People tend to become less self-centered and childish with the passage of time, and learn how to understand their own motivations and those of others. They become more capable of solving problems in their daily lives and of assuming heavy responsibilities.

As we move away from traditional forms of marriage, the question of emotional maturity becomes more central: when marriage was a vehicle for economic sur-

vival and procreation, the quality of the relationship between husband and wife was less important. A marriage
was considered sound if husband and wife carried out
their assigned roles. Today, marriage involves much
more interaction between the partners, and rests primarily on emotional compatibility. People wed for companionship, intellectual intimacy, close communication,
romantic love, and sexual pleasure, anticipating much
personal growth and fulfillment. These expectations are
more ambiguous—and difficult to satisfy—than old-style
marriage requirements; they involve qualities that can
improve with age.

Many studies have shown that age, as related to emotional maturity and personal growth, has a definite effect
on marital happiness. A couple who marries when the
man is less than twenty years old and the woman less
than eighteen has a much smaller chance of finding satisfaction in marriage than a couple ten years older. Couples
who wed as they approach their thirties have been found
to make the most rapid—and effective—marital adjust-
ments. They tend to have a better idea of what marriage
involves, and they have had ample time to observe the
marriages of others. They can profit from their earlier experiences and are more likely to select their spouse on the
basis of companionship rather than as a result of sexual
interest alone. Latecomers to matrimony also know what
it is to be a single adult and are less likely to regret
having forgone that lifestyle.

Psychologist Marcia Lasswell, studying the "best age
to marry," has determined that women who marry at age
twenty-eight or older and men who marry between
twenty-eight and thirty have the highest level of satisfaction with their marriages. Not all marriages that last are
happy ones, but marital satisfaction is closely related to
marital stability. In terms of marital longevity, the optimal age for men ranged between twenty-seven and thirty-

one and, for women, over twenty-five. Of course, prerequisites for marital stability and happiness vary with the style of marriage a couple desires and the nature of the individuals involved. But on the whole, Dr. Lasswell found that most of the evidence favors waiting until twenty-five or thirty to marry to attain both satisfaction and stability.

Divorce statistics bear out these findings: a couple who tie the knot when the man is under twenty are about three times as likely to dissolve their union in the first five years of marriage as one that weds when the man is ten years older. Marital age is also related to money and education: the more money and education a couple have, the greater the chance that their marriage will survive. A 1971 Census Bureau study showed that in marriages in which both spouses had college degrees and made $15,000 or more there was less likelihood of divorce, with marital breakups increasing as one went down the educational and socio-economic scale.

We should also keep in mind that many people in our society ripen late, and may marry when they are less mature than their years. Commentators on American life frequently point to the phenomenon of "prolonged adolescence," which can last as long as fifteen to twenty years. Contemporary society has created a whole new class of young people who depend on others for guidance and support until they are well past their teens. Extended adolescence is especially prevalent among those who need to rely on their parents or outside sources to finance college, graduate school, or other forms of advanced training. It is not uncommon to see thirty-year-olds who have never had the privileges or responsibilities of adults. Obviously, a thirty-year-old who has lingered in this phase would profit from delaying marriage and parenthood as much as someone ten years his junior.

Most people find parenthood rewarding. But they

also find that children bring tension and crisis. The birth of a baby turns two into three—transforms a husband and wife into a mother and father. Sociologists who have studied the family feel that adding a child forces as drastic a reorganization of the family unit as does removing a family member through death or divorce. Family expert E. E. LeMasters, observing the mounting pressure and responsibility that accompany parenthood, suggested that "parenthood (not marriage) marks the final transition to maturity and adult responsibility in our culture. Thus the arrival of the first child forces the young married couple to take the last painful step into the adult world."

Who is most capable of making the adjustment? It has commonly been thought that the best candidates for parenthood are young. But social scientists have found much evidence to the contrary: Corinne Nydegger of the Institute of Human Development at the University of California at Berkeley has concluded that "late is great." She found that the older fathers she studied didn't conform to the popular stereotype of the aged parent and felt less "role strain and discomfort" than fathers in their twenties. Men who became fathers during their mid-thirties and forties found the adjustment much easier than those under thirty-three. It was the younger fathers who experienced the most tension from competing family and career demands.

Older parents may be more receptive to settling down into family life. They have had plenty of time for travel and busy social schedules and may welcome the regularity that children demand. They have probably accomplished much of what they set out to do and have a better understanding of their strengths, limitations, and priorities. "They've already faced and gone through a lot of their own crises when they were in their twenties," says psychoanalyst Donald M. Kaplan. "By the time you're thirty, the question of 'Who am I?' has been answered." Older parents also have had sufficient time to establish careers and are less likely to feel that the time required to care for a child takes away from something more important.

According to Dr. Lee Salk, "Many older parents have so much to give their children—more understanding, love based on realism rather than impossible expectations. They are often more grateful for what they have than resentful about what they don't. If they are more relaxed about the structure of their own day-to-day existence, they are better able to participate in their child's life and don't regard each minor incident as a major tragedy. Or if they sense impending troubles, they are often better able to avoid them."

Recent findings have also smashed another prevalent misconception about parenthood—the role of children in divorce. During the 1930's and 1940's 60 percent of all divorcing couples were childless. This was taken as evidence that having children would save a tottering marriage. It actually meant that divorce tends to come early in marriage and the average couple of the Depression years did not begin reproducing as early as it does now. Today's divorce statistics reveal that the majority of separating couples do have children and that children can tear a marriage further apart. Studies of child spacing show a higher divorce rate for couples whose first conception occurred shortly after marriage than for those who waited before having children. Marriage counselors often advise couples to postpone parenthood until they have had time to work out the strains in their relationship. Here, too, the older couple who has waited to have children has the edge.

Today, when raising children takes up only a small portion of a couple's lifetime, delaying parenthood can be particularly beneficial to women. The pure motherhood role has come under attack from feminists and researchers concerned about its stultifying effects on women's emotional and intellectual growth. Professor Jessie Bernard believes, "From the very earliest years, girls will have to learn that . . . motherhood is going to be a relatively transient phase of their lives, that they cannot indulge themselves by investing all their emotional and intellectual resources in their children, that they cannot count on being supported all their lives simply because they are wives."

Social scientists have found that excessive concentration on the maternal role can lead to a low sense of self-esteem and vulnerability to depression when the children leave home. Women who bear children too soon have much less chance to develop an independent identity and to find other outlets for their talents. By limiting their world to the nursery, they may find themselves held back as their husband and children grow. According to fertility experts Larry Bumpass and Charles Westoff, "The longer a couple delays the occurrence of a 'wanted' birth, the more opportunity the wife has to acquire role patterns not defined in terms of early child care responsibility."

Does everything fall on the plus side for the older parent? Finances and emotional maturity are but part of the complex web of concerns prospective parents should take into account. Deciding how long to wait involves other compelling issues—medical, psychological, and social. To raise the age of childbearing is to dramatically alter patterns of reproduction and family life that have been with us for thousands of years. What does late parenthood mean—to the individual, to the family, and to society? These are the questions this book sets out to answer.

2

Career and Parenthood: What Difference Does Age Make?

"It used to be, when I first had my children, that people would ask me only, 'How can you be a good mother?' Now, and for the past five years, the most frequent question has been, 'How do you manage to be both a good mother and a good professional?'" These are the words of a late-blooming mother and senior editor who does manage to do both well. As more women pour into the labor force, the feasibility of combining work and family has become a hot topic; we can't learn enough about it from magazines, TV panels, even cocktail conversations.

The career-family issue surrounds the older parenthood phenomenon, for developing a satisfying career has been one of the prime motives for waiting to have children. The question is, what difference does it make? Does delaying parenthood help solve the problems of combining job and family? And how will it affect those who opt for the traditional parental roles?

Older Parenthood: How Can It Help?

Delaying parenthood can definitely help reduce some of the strains of working while raising children. It allows both husband and wife to complete whatever training and preparation their jobs require. I'll never forget a couple with whom I attended graduate school who had a child during their early twenties, just as they had started work on advanced degrees. They had no money for sitters and tried to make do on tuna-fish casseroles in a cramped two-room apartment. "We're managing," they said stoically, "on five hours of sleep a night." The couple who waits longer to have children usually avoids this kind of pitfall.

Most career building takes place between the ages of twenty-five and thirty-five. In demanding occupations men and women need those years to concentrate on their work. Older parents who have already developed professional reputations are more likely to feel secure in their jobs. They no longer need to prove their abilities to their colleagues and are less apt to bring their worries home. Once through the door of the house, they can devote themselves to their family.

Unfortunately, the brunt of the tensions from combining career and family has usually been borne by women. It has been common practice for the wife to drop out of work for a long period of time when the babies come. Once this happens, developing a career becomes an uphill battle. "If you cut out early in life, you just never recoup," said Claudia Dreifus, author of *Radical Lifestyles* and *Woman's Fate*. "The old pattern of working three years and dropping out careerwise at 25 is disastrous. You're competing with men who have all that time to claw their way to where they are going."

Psychologically, too, women can't become committed to a career if they have children too early. The traditional values that designate men the breadwinners and women the custodians of the household are still very potent. Unless a woman has developed a strong sense of self before she has children, she can easily be consumed by full-time motherhood.

Gail Sheehy, author of *Passages: Predictable Crises in Adult Life*, believes that in our society women don't achieve the personal growth to combine career and family roles until their thirties. "It is rarely possible for a woman to integrate marriage, career and motherhood in her twenties," she says. "It is quite possible to do so at thirty and decidedly possible at thirty-five, but before then, the *personal* integration necessary as a ballast simply hasn't a chance to develop."

When both spouses work, it is usually the husband who holds the more lucrative and prestigious job. Discriminatory hiring practices work in his favor, and generally being a bit older than his wife, he has had more time to get ahead. When the couple decides to have children, it rarely makes sense for him to stay home. Very few families are willing to forfeit a large paycheck for one that is much smaller or to gamble on a job with less security and seniority. "Why should I give up my $25,000-a-year job when my wife only makes $12,000?" the argument runs. This type of reasoning can undermine the woman's self-confidence, making her reluctant to return to work as soon as possible. And if she does make it back, she is still programmed to put her husband's job first.

Such self-negating tendencies are much less likely to develop in women whose careers are on a firm footing before they start their families. If a woman has a job on the same level of prestige, seniority, and pay as her husband, it will make no more sense for her to stay home with the children than for her spouse to. Chances are, she won't. Of course, she still has to contend with cultural pressures to keep her tied to the house, but she'll dismiss them more easily if she has a strong sense of identification with her work.

Studies have shown that women combine the demands of family and job most successfully when they find their job rewarding. They're more willing to make sacrifices to keep their job if they find it challenging and profitable. The types of positions worth fighting for are at the higher level. Women are more likely to hold such jobs if they have worked ten years or more. Many of the older mothers I interviewed believed they had a large psychological stake in remaining at work. They enjoyed their jobs and feared the loss of stimulation if they left. "It's not easy to work while the children are young," said a Wall Street attorney, "but I think I'd go crazy if I stayed home all day."

The longer a woman works, the more likely her employer is to have a vested interest in keeping her on. With enough seniority she can win special concessions that ease the career-family mix—maternity leave, flexible working hours, long vacations, enough salary to pay for household help. "I never could have had children and my job if I hadn't waited" was the consensus of the career women I interviewed.

One of the most painful problems for working women with small children has been dealing with a deep-seated sense of guilt, triggered by the question "But what will happen to the children?" Women have been given to believe that children suffer emotionally if their mothers are not available to give them constant care. At the first sign of children weeping at the doorstep, many women who do not have to go to work for financial reasons give up.

Recent pediatric theories have challenged the traditional belief that the mother must maintain a constant presence in the home to raise psychologically sound children. Even Dr. Benjamin Spock, the influential champion of full-time motherhood, has shifted position. He now admits, "I recognize that the father's responsibility is as great as the mother's" and "Both parents have an equal right to a career if they want one."

Examining the hundreds of studies of the effects of maternal employment, Dr. Mary C. Howell of Massachusetts General Hospital has concluded that "no uniformly harmful effects on family life, nor on the growth and development of the children have been demonstrated. It is concluded that conditions of employment and the attitudes of other family members probably influence the employed mother's relationship to her family by affecting her self-esteem and energy sources."

Writes Dr. Alvin N. Eden, associate clinical professor of pediatrics at New York University School of Medicine:

> In my experience and the experience of others, children of working mothers do as well as those of non-working mothers . . . If the proper surrogate mother is found, these babies grow up just as emotionally sound as do the ones without the working mother. I am firmly convinced that what babies and children need is quality care. The actual number of hours one spends with the child is not as important. What is important is how the time is spent. As far as I am concerned a working mother who comes home contented and fulfilled after a good day's work and who then spends one hour with her baby in a happy, giving frame of mind does more for her baby than the harassed, dissatisfied mother who is home all day long with her baby, but wishes she were elsewhere.

In other words, as my own pediatrician said, "If you like what you're doing, whether it is working or not, your children will be much happier than if you don't. Their happiness is dependent on your happiness." So the woman who enjoys her job should be as successful a mother as the woman who stays home full time—provided *she* likes her job. The issue hinges not on work vs. motherhood but on the mother's attitude toward work and her ability to provide appropriate child-care arrangements. Older women with a sure sense of themselves and established careers are likely to do better than younger women on both counts.

Author Jean Curtis, who studied over two hundred working mothers, found that there were times when leaving home to go to work was easier than others. Women who did not stop working had fewer problems with their children than full-time mothers who tried to resume work before their children started school. In other words, children who were accustomed to their mothers working had minimal adjustment problems and were much less likely to suffer from separation trauma—they had lived with the same situation since infancy. The older mother who is committed to keeping her job and can afford quality care for her preschooler scores another point.

The cost of child care has added to the pressure on women to stay at home. Unfortunately, very few families view child care as a business expense for both husband and wife. Most ask only if it is worthwhile for the wife to work, subtracting the cost of sitters and household help from her salary alone. This method of calculation often discourages women from working. Older women, however, are more likely to pull down salaries that can accommodate child-care arrangements. But even a working professional woman with a high-level job isn't necessarily going to come out that far ahead at first. I've heard numerous complaints of depleted paychecks from women with handsome salaries. "You know, after I finish paying taxes and the sitter," said Ellen, the bank vice-president, "I take home only $2,500." A social scientist pulling down close to $20,000 annually said, "After taxes I'm lucky if I clear $1,500 above my child-care expenses."

Yet none of the women I interviewed had any intention of staying home. Financially it still made sense to work. Close to one third of their salaries was in the form of valuable fringe benefits—life insurance, medical and pension plans—that would be forfeited by leaving their jobs. These women also realized that their child-care expenses would eventually come to an end and the size of their paycheck would go up with each year on the job. The more promising the career, the more the costs of keeping the job were a worthwhile investment.

All the older working women I interviewed preferred housekeepers to care for their children. "I really like having my children taken care of in a smaller setting than day-care centers," said Ellen. "Under one year or two years there's too much risk of infection from contact with other children."

Most of these women could afford to employ full-time household help and continued to do so when their children were in school. They had demanding jobs and a familiar complaint was: "I can't make the eight-to-six schedule for day-care centers as I have to work late." When their jobs involved traveling, they relied on housekeepers who lived in. Usually the housekeepers took charge of cleaning and cooking as well as of the children.

The most frequent problem of the working women I met was finding a reliable surrogate willing to stay with their families for several years. Other drawbacks of housekeepers—"They are the ones who bring the sweets and candy to the kids." "Many babysitters aren't keen on taking care of three children—one or two are about all they want to handle. And if there's more than one child, the sitter usually picks a favorite." "Often the housekeeper's family problems become your problems, too." But because of the nature of their jobs, the older career women I interviewed still felt some form of flexible one-to-one arrangement worked best.

Suppose a full-time housekeeper is too troublesome or expensive? Once the children are past infancy, day care can be an attractive alternative. (Many day-care centers accept only children who are toilet-trained.) Children over two and a half years become less dependent on their parents. They enjoy spending time with other youngsters. Well-run day-care centers with properly trained staff can give children unique developmental advantages—they impart early learning and social skills that can't be acquired easily at home. Parents with reasonably regular work schedules should be able to take advantage of this type of arrangement.

An alternative to day care or full-time household help is family day care. In some areas federal and state programs pay selected women to serve as surrogate mothers for up to six children in their own homes. The homes are licensed day-care centers and the surrogate mothers are paid on a sliding scale by the city and parent. This type of setting is less institutional than a formal day-care center and gives the child the benefits of a one-to-one relationship.

To compensate for spending so much of the day away from home, the career women I spoke with made it a point to be with their children as much as possible during non-working hours. Generally they did this by cutting down on outside activities and entertaining. "I didn't really have time to socialize," said a social worker. "It's just not possible for a working mother." The Wall Street attorney told me, "Henry and I try to plan our social life around our son. We look forward to playing with him when we come home at night. We take him with us when we eat out. Sure, we've given up friends and parties, but you can't count on friends that much, anyway. They always come and go."

One busy couple in real estate said, "We read about

these people who work and have children and entertain a lot and cook gourmet meals and we wonder, how do they do it?" Even with all the advantages of waiting for children, delaying parenthood can't turn working mothers into Wonder Women. But by waiting, career-minded couples did have more time to work out their list of priorities. They knew they wanted to work; they knew they wanted children. If something had to give—social life, travel, reading Agatha Christie in bed—they were mature enough to accept the sacrifice.

Job and Children: What Delayed Parenthood Can't Help

On the whole, delaying parenthood in order to build job status helps couples combine work and family. But it's not a panacea for all family-career problems, and in some situations, it adds to the tension.

A number of the women I interviewed were pioneers of sorts. Many occupied high-level jobs that traditionally had been reserved for men or for women who were childless or single. In their office usually it was the secretaries who had children and then left their jobs permanently. As a result, their firms had no program for maternity benefits or maternity leave.

By working up to high-level jobs which they had no intention of leaving, the career women who became pregnant were breaking long-standing precedents. Their colleagues were not used to working closely with pregnant women and occasionally made unnecessary comments like, "Oh, Ellen, you're so *big!* How are you going to *manage?*" One woman in financial research had no trouble with her co-workers but was made uncomfortable by her personnel office. The administrator in charge of maternity leaves said, "Even if you've made them vice-president they still don't come right back. This won't be a four-month maternity leave but an eight-month leave."

An editor at an educational publishing house noticed that her male colleagues stopped asking her to lunch after her pregnancy went beyond seven months.

One publishing executive was the first woman in her firm to take a paid maternity leave. That was fifteen years ago; fortunately, maternity benefits and maternity leaves are becoming more commonplace. The older women who recently had children report much less trouble securing time off to recover from childbirth. Some have been able to spend three or four months working at home with pay. But until more women join the ranks, the women in top positions who want to have children will be waging a lonely battle.

Attitudes toward career women with families have changed more rapidly in some parts of the country than others. The atmosphere's more congenial in a city such as New York than one that is culturally less advanced. "I would have had a much harder time in Pittsburgh," said the banking executive. "There the men don't take you as seriously."

In certain types of careers, work and parenthood just don't mix. Liking children is insufficient grounds for having them—you must be able to spend enough time with them to play a meaningful parental role. I know a number of male attorneys and businessmen who work until nine or ten every evening, plus Saturdays and Sundays. If they have children, they heap all the family responsibilities on their wives. If their wives have similar schedules, they just don't procreate. The same is true for couples whose jobs involve traveling a large part of the year. For this kind of problem, delaying parenthood won't be an answer. Any couple contemplating children, whether they are older or not, would do well to look closely at the flexibility of their time schedules. If work takes up a rigid eighty hours a week, and if you strongly cherish your limited free time, having a baby will surely overload the circuits. Some people have been able to get around this by switching jobs or moving into related but less demanding fields. One attorney friend in real estate found her job kept her in the office until ten every night. "I had no time for my children, or myself for that matter," she said. She was able to find another job as the house attorney for a large corporation where the schedule got her home by six.

A couple's success in working out some type of job-family arrangement will also depend a great deal on their ability to adjust to multiple sets of demands. I remember a psychologist who counseled shaky marriages telling me, "A marriage just won't work unless a couple can *cooperate*." The statement seemed a bit trite but nonetheless rang true. And it applies even more to couples who add children to the equation. Whether a working couple with children is young or older, their ability to share responsibilities at home can make or break the relationship. All too often, it is the wives who are saddled with the responsibility for children and housework, the old "double work" story. Even with housekeepers there are certain tasks only a parent can perform—staying up at night to feed a young infant or to tend a sick child, visiting the pediatrician, tidying the house on the house-keeper's day off, shopping for groceries. All the women I interviewed had husbands who were supportive of their work, but only a few had spouses who actively pitched in on the home front. The rest of the women managed very much like author Letitia Baldridge—they learned the fine art of juggling and coped.

Delaying parenthood gives women an edge as jugglers, but much more is needed to change what is fundamentally at stake, the persistence of outdated definitions of male and female roles. If women are to achieve equality with men, we need a society where men have as much responsibility for the children and the home as women, where combining career and family is an issue for *both* parents. Some of the emerging generation of parents are moving toward this vision. Observes sociology professor Cynthia Epstein, a leading authority on women's issues: "Many men are changing, and not just because of ideology. With growing numbers of divorces they've had to assume more responsibility for the children and are experiencing parenthood in a new way. And the climate of the times is different—even those who don't like it still feel they have to take part." Delaying parenthood has worked to better the position of women, but true equality between the sexes will require further transformation of our institutions and values.

What If You Don't Want to Work?

The case for working and raising a family has not demolished the argument for staying at home. Those who sympathize with the women's movement would put it this way: "It's wrong to make a woman feel guilty if she wants to leave the house and her children to take a job, but it's equally wrong to make a woman feel she has to justify staying home." Not everyone wants to leave their mark on the world through their work, including some of the women who have delayed parenthood. "I'm not the kind who would give up everything for a job," said one woman who had her first child in her late thirties. "I also want to be able to spend a lot of time with my family and keep up my other interests."

Some women are intensely devoted to both children and career but just haven't found an arrangement to combine both that they like. One professor said, "I had other friends who didn't give up their jobs and scorned me for being devoted to my family. Mothering has been an important focus in my life. But in terms of my career it has hurt me—there is no question about that. I did a lot of reading at home and I think I broadened myself much more that way and emerged a better scholar from it. But I did lose valuable time in my career. If I hadn't stayed home I would have been a full professor with tenure by now. On the other hand, I'm delighted with my results—a nineteen-year-old son and eighteen-year-old daughter. They're sound human beings. I'm happy I made the commitment to them."

It may be difficult to find suitable child-care facilities or the type of parental surrogate who inspires trust. How one raises children is a highly individual matter. Many women who stay home out of choice do not want to leave the job of "molding another human being" to someone else. Or they feel that their children would suffer without Brownie Scouts, after-school trips to the library, or music lessons, activities that a full-time parent can most easily arrange.

There are women who have already fulfilled their career goals and are ready to move on. One former journalist who opted to stay home with her child after working ten years said, "I feel more liberated now because I don't have to prove anything any more." And an older woman who has waited for a child may feel it's her last chance to play a mother's role—and wants to play it to the hilt.

Delaying parenthood can be beneficial to the woman who wants to stay at home, too. It gives her a chance to find out who she is and to determine how children will fit into her life. She may turn into a full-time mother, but her identity is unlikely to be forced into a narrow motherhood mold.

There's no reason why older women can't enjoy full-time motherhood. But they may have trouble adapting to spending most of their time at home after so many years of independence. A former personnel manager who married and had children in her thirties complained, "I really can't take it, and frankly, I'm bored. My children are four and six and not very interesting to talk to. I've been too used to communicating with adults."

Staying home may spare a mother from huffing and puffing to work, but it allows for little peace and quiet. The more accustomed one is to the world outside the home, the more drastic the impact of rescheduling for children. A Detroit study of 217 mothers asked, "How is a woman's life changed by having children?" The most common response: "Lack of freedom . . . it ties you down to the house." The most negative replies came from college-educated women. An older woman's maturity and desire for a child may help her deal with her isolation. But if she chooses full-time motherhood, she will still have a difficult transition to make.

A distinct status shift takes place when a woman accustomed to bringing home a paycheck becomes a "housewife"; unfortunately, the term has a slightly derogatory connotation. Our culture puts women in a double bind. It glorifies motherhood but looks down on work that doesn't pay.

"Though we give lip service to the idea that mother-work is worthy, hardly anyone really believes it," says sociologist Jessie Bernard. "Most of us agree with Philip Slater's dictum that the housewife is a nobody. Mothering has 'use value' but not 'exchange value.' The mother of young children whose admittedly indispensable activities devoted to their care leave her exhausted does not fall into the category of worker because her activities are, by definition, not gainful."

The position of the housewife has deteriorated further under the impact of feminist values. Wrote David M. Elsner in *The Wall Street Journal*, "A middle class woman who *doesn't* have an educational or career goal is likely to be looked down upon in some communities."

Estimates show that a full-time housewife performs

a variety of services which, at the rate charged on the open market, would net her $14,000 a year. But the full-time mother isn't paid for her services and becomes totally dependent financially on her husband. And she must come to terms with the lingering belief that somehow being a housewife isn't real work. An older woman who has developed a sense of accomplishment from working on her own may find the downward shift to housewife a painful one.

I found that the older women who continued to work after their children were born had less chance of being limited to the company of mothers who were much younger. Through their work they were able to retain the same set of friends and social contacts. They generally left their housekeepers to deal with the "mothers in the park." An older mother is more apt to rub against women from another generation or lifestyle if she spends most of her time at home.

Unless she is dead set on staying home, I would recommend that an older mother try an experimental leave of absence. This can be in the form of a maternity leave—paid or unpaid—or an arrangement with her employer to take six months off before making a final decision about continuing work. This plan allows a woman to try out full-time motherhood to see if it suits her needs and temperament. Just as many women will find they can't handle both children and work, others will discover they can't tolerate spending all their time at home.

If plans for leaving work for a longer period of time are definite, older women in particular should try to develop outside activities. It's a good time to indulge in interests that did not fit into a full-time working schedule—classical guitar lessons, for example, or classes in art appreciation, pottery, or painting, or that course in Egyptian history you've always wanted to take. Setting years aside for young children doesn't mean that one's personal growth must stand still. A number of women told me they used this period in their lives to develop the creative side of their character.

While children are too young for school, a woman's schedule may not allow for a full-time job. But it can most likely accommodate day or evening classes at a local college or university. By using part-time sitters, a woman can return to school to upgrade her job skills or prepare for a new career—obtaining a B.A. or an advanced degree in social work, acquiring an M.B.A. or credits in accounting, learning how to use a computer. American education has developed an extensive system for part-time and continuing education. Many schools now have B.A. and postgraduate-degree programs for older students during evenings and weekends.

A number of large universities, such as the University of Minnesota, the University of Missouri, and Syracuse University, operate Continuing Education Centers for women. The University of Michigan's Center for Continuing Education for Women has awarded fellowships to those ranging from age twenty-one to forty-three. George Washington University has off-campus programs in suburban Maryland and Virginia, and Purdue University has created a "Span" program for older women.

Some schools have even developed M.B.A.'s for women or training programs that prepare women for jobs in management. U.C.L.A.'s university extension program offers a series of management courses attended by about six thousand women each year. Katharine Gibbs, noted for its secretarial classes, now runs evening management courses for women, and Adelphi University has a special Management for Women program.

Some schools schedule classes during the times most convenient for housewives. The New School for Social Research in Manhattan holds courses during breakfast and lunch, evenings and weekends. WIFE (Women Interested in Further Education) of Mercer County Community College in Trenton, New Jersey, features a two-year series of courses between 10 A.M. and 2 P.M. Marymount Manhattan College has weekend programs in business management, psychology, and sociology.

Many colleges and universities have also opened on-campus day-care centers. About 350 campus day-care centers are operating throughout the country, twenty-five in the New York metropolitan area alone. They are represented by the National Campus Child Care Council in Arlington, Virginia.

You can find out about part-time programs in your area from these sources: the publications of the Committee on Continuing Education of Women, Adult Education Association, 810 18th Street N.W., Washington, D.C. 20036; "On-Campus/Off-Campus Degree Programs for Part-time Students," issued by the National University Extension Association, Suite 360, 1 Dupont Circle, Washington, D.C. 20036; *The New York Times Guide to Continuing Education in America*, published by Quadrangle Books; *The Weekend Education Source Book* by Wilbur Cross, published by Harper's Magazine Press; and *Continuing Education Programs and Services for Women*, published by the Women's Bureau of the U.S. Department of Labor, Washington, D.C. 20210. The National Center for Educational Brokering, 405 Oak Street, Syracuse, New York 13203, lists educational brokering centers that provide information and counseling services for course offerings in at least twenty-five states.

The Women's Bureau of the Department of Labor forecasts rapid expansion of openings for women between now and 1980 in employment counseling, market research, occupational therapy, physical therapy, programming, systems analysis, and urban planning. The number of jobs is expected to rise for accountants, architects, chemists, civil engineers, dentists, dieticians, economists, electrical engineers, industrial engineers, life scientists, mathematicians, medical-record librarians, speech pathologists, registered nurses, statisticians, and veterinarians. Information on occupational openings for women can be found in *Publications of the Women's Bureau* (Leaflet No. 10), Women's Bureau, U.S. Department of Labor, Washington, D.C. 20210, or in books such as *There's Always a Right Job for Every Woman* by Roberta Roesch and *The Woman's Work Book* by Karin Abarbanel and Gonnie McClung Siegel.

If a conventional job won't meet your need for independence and flexibility, the years at home can lay a foundation for your own business. The financial and business climate (under some prodding from the women's movement) has become more receptive to female-run enterprises. Growing numbers of women are striking out on their own.

Some women have built successful businesses run from their home—shopping and plant-care services; catering; exercise classes. More ambitious projects require careful planning. The *Illustrated Woman's Almanac* has devoted one of its "handbooks" to "Your Own Business." It includes how-to's for new entrepreneurs and a checklist of business skills. The Small Business Administration also issues numerous publications on how to start and run businesses. Claudia Jessup and Genie Chipps have written *The Woman's Guide to Starting a Business*.

Part-time work has been hailed as the answer for the woman who wants to make career and family as smooth a combination as possible. Lois Hoffman and Ivan Nye, authors of *The Employed Mother in America*, believe part-time work to be "an unusually successful adaptation to the conflict between the difficulties of being a full-time housewife and the strain of combining this role with full-time employment." But they admit that good part-time work is difficult to find and, even under the best conditions, pays at a lower rate than the same task full-time. Part-time work generally can't offer the same degree of job security or fringe benefits as a full-time position. Most part-time schedules are also geared toward the convenience of the employer, not the part-time worker.

"A lot of women complain to me after they've left high-level jobs, 'If I could only find some interesting part-time work,'" says a top editor. What about freelance work? It often has the same financial drawbacks as part-time and the supply of freelance jobs is limited. Ruth Lembeck's *380 Part-time Jobs for Women* discusses possibilities in various fields and can give an idea of the requisite skills, experience, and salary levels involved. Part-time work is also explored in detail in *How to Go to Work When Your Husband Is Against It, Your Children Aren't Old Enough and There's Nothing You Can Do Anyhow* by Felice N. Schwartz, Margaret H. Schifter, and Susan H. Gillotti.

Going Back to Work: Does It Work Out for the Older Parent?

In recent years our society has become more flexible about job patterns. We need not be locked for the rest of our lives in occupations we chose during our youth; it has become increasingly common to change careers mid-stream. To a certain extent, this has been true for women who have made full-time motherhood their first "job." The United States labor market has made some allowance for women returning to work after their children are grown or in school.

How well women fare when they return, however, will depend on their age, their skills, and the amount of time they have been out of the work force. In general, as a person grows older, attractive jobs become harder to obtain. "The older you get, the more difficult it is to return to work," says Professor Epstein. "The whole age-grading structure and set of attitudes about jobs in this society works against that process. And it's not just for women—men have that problem, too. People don't want to invest in someone who is going to be there only a few years."

According to John Cullinan, head of the Illinois State Employment Bureau in Waukegan, "Women going back to work are constantly hearing that they don't have enough experience. Companies can get individuals out of college knowing they don't have experience, but they can bring them up 'the company way.' With older women, this is more difficult."

Observes a bank vice-president, "I think anyone forty years old is going to have trouble finding a job—period. There are so many younger people with advanced degrees looking for work now, you're going to have a hard time if you're over thirty. Going back to work will be easier for a secretary than for someone who wants a high-level position, especially in a field like mine, economics, where the technology and ideas are changing all the time. And it's still harder for a woman to go back to work than a guy who has done the same thing."

Those attractive jobs will move even further from reach if, on top of her age, a woman has been out of the work force for a long time. "Many women have been out of the work force for so long, they have been so isolated in the family unit, that it is tough for them to re-enter the job market," says Dr. Lenora Mundt of the University of Washington, co-founder of a Seattle women's counseling center. "When they first start calling on employers, they get a feeling of inadequacy, especially in terms of what their skills are worth financially."

According to William Lawson, an official at the California Employment Development Division, "Breakthroughs by women in new occupations are widely publicized in the news media, but their numbers are small. Most women in California just don't have these opportunities. They have not accumulated as much experience at a given age as a man."

A Labor Department study has found that many mothers returning to work wind up with jobs lower in occupational status than their original jobs before they married. Almost one third of the women who re-entered the labor market between the ages of thirty and thirty-three have been unable to get beyond the same jobs they held when they were younger. Labor market analysts foresee little change in this situation over the next decade.

The occupational structure for women returning to work has operated on the assumption that most will complete their families by their early thirties. (The majority of American mothers see their youngest child off to school before they are thirty-two.) At that point, finding an attractive job is hard enough. But what if a woman doesn't begin having children until then? Obviously she'll have a much rougher time job hunting if she stays home long enough to see her children in school.

Employment counselors have found that re-entering the work force has been especially difficult for women thirty-five and over. And returning to work when you're older can add to friction on the job. "People who are older and return to work may have intense conflicts," says Professor Epstein. "They're older but are given junior positions working with junior people. Yet they somehow expect to be treated according to their age."

Is being older any advantage at all for women returning to work? Let's assume you aren't too old to be employable. It has been established that an educated woman with the proper training and job experience will fare better in the job market than one without such qualifications. "From the point of view of getting back to work and having interesting and well-paid work, you do far better to put off having children until you are thirty-two and have all your higher credentials," stated Ann Dally, a British author, practicing psychiatrist—and mother of six.

Studies of mothers returning to work have found that they have been held back by their own lack of self-assurance. Generally the "lack of confidence" phenomenon hits hardest among women who only worked for a few years before starting their families. With too many years confined to the home and too little practice relating to other adults, they tend to underrate their abilities and skills in a work situation. This can make them shrink from the challenge of a demanding job or any job at all. A woman who has put in over a decade of work before motherhood is less likely to have this problem, provided she doesn't stay away from her job too long. With the right training and skills, an older mother returning to work can turn her age into an asset.

If you're older and want to stay home while the children are young, but eventually want to return to work, what is the best course of action? First, I'd consider holding the number of years away from a job to the minimum. I know one woman in her mid-fifties who stayed home too long. She is brilliant, articulate, dynamic, a Phi Beta Kappa graduate of an Ivy League school, with writing experience and her M.A. from a leading school of journalism. For the past five years she has tried to find work in her field and has yet to come up with a job. Try to avoid this plight.

In preparation for a return to work, I'd also recommend keeping in close touch with your field. Try to maintain some relationship with your former employer and colleagues, and read up on the latest developments in trade or professional papers and journals. This is especially important in lines of work that are sophisticated and rapidly changing. It may be possible to keep active at home by working on a freelance basis. If you're considering changing fields, this period at home should be used to plan out new career goals. You may wish to consult special counseling centers for women that have been set up in many states. These may be private or publicly subsidized. Local chapters of NOW (National Organization for Women), WEAL (Women's Equity Action League), and the Women's Political Caucus often provide information and referrals for counseling services.

Successful re-entry into the labor force—at any age—will also depend on the nature of the job market. The larger the supply of qualified candidates, the more a woman's age is apt to be held against her. A woman aged forty or forty-five may find job hunting relatively easy with an M.B.A., impossible with a Ph.D. in English history. And the availability of promising jobs also varies in each geographic area. The same set of qualifications in a forty-five-year-old woman could net a high-paying position in a boom town like Houston, Texas; a mediocre one in economically depressed Boston or New York; or in San Francisco, where Ph.D.'s wait on tables, no job at all.

Each woman puts her own value on her career. If she has other consuming interests besides her work, she should be free to pursue them. The main point is that her potentialities not be limited by a constricting motherhood role. Arthur Campbell, deputy director of the Center for Population Research at the National Institute of Child Health and Development, has said, "A girl pregnant at age sixteen has 90 percent of her life script written for her." By delaying parenthood, women have more of a chance to develop a set of options in the way they lead their lives. We could say, "A woman pregnant at age thirty-six writes 90 percent of her life script herself."

3

The Reproductive Time Clock: When Does It Run Out?

In this country the age of thirty is commonly perceived as some sort of dangerous turning point. In youth culture, it conveniently marks off the people you can't trust. Singles start getting the shakes about spending their fourth decade alone. And women contemplating having children worry that their reproductive time clock is about to run out.

I can still vividly recall a conversation with two of our close friends. "This is the year," Steve announced over cocktails, "when we have to decide if we are going to have children. Otherwise it will be too late." His wife had just turned thirty-one. "I was always told," confessed another friend, "that it's okay to have kids when you're twenty-eight or twenty-nine and maybe thirty, but after that the chances of mongolism and things like that go up drastically."

There is a prevalent belief that couples who postpone having children until they are past thirty threaten the health of both mother and child. Women's magazines, which invariably depict mothers as young things fresh out of high school or college, and even popular handbooks on pregnancy, have bombarded the public with vignettes such as the following:

> I learned the value of not postponing childbearing from a patient several years ago. When I first saw her she was thirty-four and had been twelve years married. She was a department store buyer and so engrossed in her career that she could never afford the time to start a family. When she suddenly realized age was catching up, she got pregnant very efficiently, and excitedly came to see me. On examination, I found that she had a fibroid tumor of the uterus many times the size of her early pregnancy and when, because of complications, the whole uterus had to be removed, leaving her forever childless, she kept sobbing to me in a kind of chant, "Why didn't someone tell me you should have children while young?"

Cultural pressure for young motherhood is not necessarily relieved by consulting a gynecologist. I remember another friend who returned home from her annual checkup in a state of rage. She was only twenty-seven but her doctor said to her, "Well, Marsha, it's time for you to have a baby."

Such experiences have reinforced the prevailing fears that older parents are penalized by defective children or difficult pregnancies. This kind of thinking frightened many couples into having children before they were ready. True, the optimal time for reproduction in both male and female is in their twenties. But does this mean that having children is incompatible with advancing years? Just how great are the risks of age? Can couples past their reproductive peak calculate the chances they will take? And is there anything they can do to make childbearing a success?

Before those past twenty-nine reach for the panic button, let's look closely at the facts. In reacting to an older pregnancy, the first thing that comes to most people's mind is the increased possibility of bearing a deformed child. But, believe it or not, with today's obstetrical tools, the most tricky part may be getting that pregnancy started.

Age and Fertility

Fertility, the capacity to conceive and bear children, declines in men and women after they reach thirty. Most women hit their reproductive peak between the ages of twenty-four and twenty-six. Their fertility declines slowly during their thirties but drops rapidly during their forties. As they approach menopause it is almost zero, and there are very few children born to women over fifty.

Male fertility likewise falls after the mid-twenties, but more gradually than that of females. Although men do not face the same reproductive time limit as women (a rare few have fathered children during their nineties), they do not escape the effects of age—a man over forty will not have the same fatherhood potential as one in his twenties.

A couple's ability to produce a child depends on how age and other factors affect both partners' reproductive systems. In other words, as Dr. Sherwin A. Kaufman, gynecologist and medical consultant for Planned Parenthood of New York City, points out, "Pregnancy is always the result of the *combined* fertility of husband and wife." A highly fertile man, for instance, may be able to produce children with a woman of relatively low fertility; another man with lower fertility may be entirely unsuccessful impregnating the same woman.

It has been estimated that 15 percent of all couples in the United States have problems conceiving a child. Fertility experts have calculated that 30 to 40 percent of the time the man is responsible. In many cases, barrenness results from the combined difficulties of both partners. For a pregnancy to "take," the structural, chemical, and timing mechanisms of both male and female reproductive systems must be properly coordinated individually and with each other.

Obstetrician-gynecologist William Sweeney III, author of *Woman's Doctor*, has put it bluntly: "There's more to fertility than screwing." Both partners must be in good general health, with their endocrine systems providing the appropriate stimulation to their sexual organs. In the woman, at least one ovary must be capable of releasing healthy eggs at the proper time for implantation in the uterus. Her fallopian tubes must be open to receive sperm and to allow the fertilized egg to pass freely into the uterus; the lining of the uterus must be ready for implantation of the embryo. Even after implantation in the uterine wall, a fertilized egg will usually not survive unless it is genetically and embryologically normal. Generally 15 percent of a woman's eggs are completely unfertilizable and another 25 percent when fertilized will spontaneously abort. A man must be able to produce healthy sperm sufficient in number and driving force to propel themselves up the uterus to meet the ovum in the fallopian tubes. The sperm must also be compatible with the chemical secretions of the woman's reproductive tract.

Anything that upsets the complicated and delicate balance involved in the production of sperm and eggs and their interaction lowers the chances of conception. According to Dr. Albert Decker, medical director of the New York Fertility Research Foundation, "The husband may have a little trouble, the wife may have a little trouble. Two little troubles make a big trouble." Age adds to the "trouble" by lowering the efficiency of both male and female systems.

How does this happen? The effects of aging in men are less dramatic than in women but can nevertheless hamper their reproductive ability. Older men, especially those over fifty, put out less of the hormone testosterone and tend to have fewer and less active sperm than in their youth. Their capacity for repeated orgasm within a short period of time begins to fall off rapidly before they are twenty and they grow slower in sexual arousal and response. As sexual relations become less frequent, the chances of conception go down. Dr. Decker, observing that "age can affect male sexual function" and that "older men have more problems in this area," reports that the New York Fertility Research Foundation has had to recommend many older men to sex therapists to deal with their problems.

Prior to menopause, the major effect of age on women appears to be in the process of ovulation and the hormonal changes associated with it. As women approach menopause, they ovulate, or produce eggs for reproduction, less frequently. It has been estimated that women forty to forty-five ovulate in 75 percent of their menstrual cycles and women over forty-six in only 60 percent. Medical researchers have speculated that this may be due to the depletion of oocytes (immature egg cells) over time, a process which begins even before a baby girl is born. By the time a woman is fifty years old, she may have almost no oocytes left in her ovaries.

Aging may also disrupt normal ovulation by altering the pattern of secretion of sex hormones. A delay in ovulation in which the egg lingers longer than the fourteenth day of the menstrual cycle before being released increases the chances of overripening. Such "bad eggs" are often genetically defective or incapable of fertilization. Changes in the timing of ovulation may affect implantation of fertilized eggs in the uterus, too.

Fertilized eggs that are defective or improperly attached to the uterus are a major cause of miscarriage.

About one in six pregnancies ends spontaneously, usually within the first few weeks after conception. The risk of miscarriages increases after a woman turns thirty, and after she is thirty-five it's about three times that of a woman in her twenties.

Advancing years also tend to aggravate conditions such as fibroid tumors and endometriosis, which can cut down on female fertility. Fibroids are benign growths composed primarily of fibrous and muscular tissue and are located in, or attached to, the uterus. They range from the size of a pea to that of a grapefruit and occur in 40 percent of all women over forty years old. Small fibroids may have no symptoms and generally do not hinder pregnancy. However, the larger growths can impinge on the fallopian tubes and cause infertility. Fibroids located inside the uterus may also interfere with implantation of the fertilized egg. Surgery, often involving hysterectomy, or removal of the uterus, is frequently performed on large fibroids that produce too much bleeding or pain.

Endometriosis, though less common, is more difficult to treat and diagnose. Cells of the endometrium, or lining of the uterus, manage to find their way outside the uterus, lodging on the ovaries, fallopian tubes, or ligaments of the pelvic cavity. There they bleed every month like the inside of the uterus. The blood is trapped internally where it can clot and scar a woman's organs, causing considerable pain and, frequently, sterility. Endometriosis is sometimes controlled by hormonal treatment or use of the Pill, thus arresting the activity of the ovaries. And suspension of menstrual periods during pregnancy may put the condition in permanent remission. But none of these measures is a surefire cure for endometriosis, and they can't reverse the damage to a woman's reproductive organs that has already occurred.

Couples who plan to wait a number of years before

having children should be aware of the possible long-term effects of contraceptives on their fertility. Condoms and diaphragms are neutral. But both the Pill and the IUD, which interact with the chemical and physical mechanisms of a woman's reproductive tract, may eventually curtail her ability to conceive. The Pill blocks production of ovarian hormones, so that ovulation cannot take place. If a woman stays on the Pill from, say, her late teens to her thirties, she will have suppressed the function of her ovaries for over a decade. Can they easily return to normal? Dr. Decker has observed that the fertility of women who have been on the Pill for some time is considerably reduced. "I have found many post-Pill ovulatory disturbances among women who took the Pill for five to seven years," he says. Moreover, women with menstrual irregularities prior to taking the Pill—who probably have irregular ovulation and therefore reduced fertility to start with—may find these difficulties exacerbated when they go off it.

Barbara Seaman, who has documented *The Doctor's Case Against the Pill,* found that the Pill stopped some women's menstrual cycles altogether. "It is no longer just a vague worry but an established fact that a certain number of women simply do not start having their periods again after they stop taking the pill. Others have irregular or scanty periods. In either case they may find that they cannot conceive. They are sterile," she says.

Women frequently experience a six-month wait between stopping the Pill and the onset of ovulation. Many gynecologists advise their patients to stop the Pill three months before trying to become pregnant to allow their systems time to return to their original state. And it is common practice to encourage women to go off the Pill every couple of years.

The IUD, which also distorts the natural functioning of a woman's body, is thought to interfere with fertility. It works by irritating the lining of the uterus to prevent implantation of a fertilized egg. The IUD user is thus subjecting her uterus to constant irritation, which may over the years cause irreparable harm. Dr. Decker has also noticed that an appreciable number of women using IUD's had difficulty conceiving.

Since no contraceptive is 100 percent effective, the woman who wants to delay pregnancy for a number of years may have to resort to abortion. Since legalization, the abortion procedure has become inexpensive and safe, but it, too, can affect fertility. Some medical researchers believe that repeated abortions increase the chances for miscarriage or certain abnormalities in later pregnancies. Fertility can also suffer from exposure over the years to various inflammatory infections such as VD, or the cumulative effects of drugs, radiation, and other environmental influences.

Suppose a couple wishes to wait until their mid- or late thirties to have children. Is there some way they can calculate the risk to their fertility? To date the only proof of fertility is fertility itself—a successful pregnancy. One of the most common mistakes that men and women make, according to Dr. Decker, is to assume that nothing is wrong with their ability to reproduce. "Everyone feels they are fertile," he says, "until they try having a baby."

Dr. Decker recommends that if a man and woman do want to wait they should have a "minimal type" fertility survey while they are still young to see if anything is grossly wrong. "The first thing a couple should do is have their fertility potential estimated." A man can generally go to a urologist, who will examine his general health, physical condition, and quality of sperm. A woman should try to find a gynecologist interested in fertility problems who is prepared to spend time discussing her needs. If she fails to find a suitable gynecologist, she should go to a fertility specialist.

For the man, analysis of semen and general state of health gives some indication of what his fertility will be in the future. However, he should not assume his condition will remain stable for ten years, since considerable degeneration can take place. A woman's fertility is considered much more difficult to assess. "The only way," Dr. Decker says, "is to expose her body to sperm." But she can be on guard for several signs of potential fertility problems—irregular or painful menstrual periods, periodic pelvic infections, or a touch of endometriosis. As Dr. Kaufman points out, "A woman who at thirty has unusually good fertility is not likely to 'drop off' significantly at thirty-five, whereas one who was borderline in fertility at thirty is very likely to be subfertile a few years later." Many physicians advise couples over the age of thirty-five to go for professional help if they do not produce a pregnancy after trying for six months.

Most infertility specialists belong to the American Fertility Society. Couples who think they need treatment can obtain names of members in their area by writing to the Office of the Director, American Fertility Society, 1801 Ninth Avenue South, Birmingham, Alabama 35205. Hospitals with strong ob-gyn facilities or teaching hospitals generally have experts on fertility problems on their staff. There are also fertility clinics in many cities in the United States. These can be located by writing to the Planned Parenthood Federation of America, 810 Seventh Avenue, New York, N.Y. 10019.

Treatment begins with a diagnostic search and survey. This includes an examination of the man's and woman's general health and medical history, along with details concerning their marital relationship, sexual habits, birth-control practices, and the woman's menstrual cycle. Both partners are subjected to a battery of tests to determine which factor—such as semen quality, ovulation, blockage of the fallopian tubes, or even psychological problems—is responsible for the impasse.

According to Dr. Decker, the seminal factor, involving sperm production, and the ovarian factor, involving defective ovulation, are most likely to cause more problems with advancing age.

If necessary, after testing, the man can be treated to build up his general health, by such measures as improved diet and physical exercise. The physician will survey the function of the thyroid, pituitary, and adrenal glands and can prescribe corrective medication for thyroid deficiency. About one third of the cases of sperm blockage can be relieved by surgery, but there is little that can be done for cases where no sperm are being produced at all. The New York Fertility Research Foundation has found, however, that older men do very well in operative treatment for large varicose veins of the scrotal sac that slow down sperm activity.

A woman with ovulatory disorders is generally treated with clomiphene citrate—the "fertility pill," made up of synthetic chemicals that stimulate the ovaries to produce eggs—or by Pergonal (human pituitary gonadotrophin), extracted from the urine of postmenopausal women, which is the drug primarily responsible for the recent rash of multiple births. But according to Dr. Decker, these treatments—which have a conception rate of 30 to 50 percent—will be somewhat less effective in older women.

What happens if none of these measures works? Modern medicine still has no antidote for the psychological problems that set in when a couple finds they can't have the child they have longed for—feelings of grief, inadequacy, mutual suspicion, embarrassment, even damaged sexual performance. Fertility experts have found older couples especially frustrated by repeated failures at conception, pressured by the realization that their time is about to run out. Such problems can't be glossed over lightly.

There aren't too many answers for the man and woman at the end of the line who have found out conclusively that they can't have children. If the male factor is involved, they can try artificial insemination. In the future, women with defective fallopian tubes may be able to have their eggs fertilized in a test tube for implantation into the uterus. When everything else fails, there's the possibility of adoption. However, the pool of children available for adoption is shrinking fast and eligibility requirements are more stringent. Many agencies refuse to place a child in a home where the wife works full time. And the couple who don't find out about their infertility problem until the later years may be past the age to qualify as adoptive parents.

So the couple contemplating older parenthood should be sure to take their fertility into account. Some couples who delay having children will have no trouble conceiving at all. By waiting so long, the ones with a serious fertility problem to begin with will have passed the point of no return. In most cases when fertility is weakened by age, however, conceiving a child will probably take more time—instead of several months, perhaps several years. This delay can be frustrating psychologically and makes it difficult to really plan a pregnancy.

Birth Defects and Parental Age

Once past the fertility hurdle, the picture for older parents brightens. Through recent advances in obstetrics the other aspects of an older pregnancy have become much easier to handle. Today, older parents' chances for a successful pregnancy and healthy child have never been better.

The greatest fear that haunted older men and women who wanted children was the possibility of bearing babies who were severely retarded and/or deformed. Statistically, they do have a somewhat greater chance of producing a child with congenital abnormalities. This is especially true of genetic disorders. Scientists have speculated that this is due to defects in both sperm and egg as the father's and mother's reproductive systems degenerate over time. Older mothers are more likely to produce bad eggs. They may be overripe from waiting four decades in the ovaries before being released for fertilization. Or they may have suffered from delayed ovulation, so that they are not fertilized until they are about to disintegrate. The genetic material in eggs and sperm may not duplicate and divide normally when they are being produced in either male or female tracts or when they combine during conception. Genetic mutations are also caused by exposure to radiation from natural sources such as cosmic rays and chemicals in the earth, and manmade sources such as X rays, radar, and atomic energy. The older the individual, the greater the amount of radiation that has bombarded his or her body.

The most widespread genetic defect associated with aging parents is Down's syndrome, or mongolism. Mongolism affects about one in six hundred babies and is the most common cause of mental retardation in this country. Many mongoloids suffer from serious heart defects, and until recently, most died before reaching adulthood. With very low intelligence, they often needed to be institutionalized.

Scientists now know that 97 percent of the cases of Down's syndrome are caused by the presence of an extra chromosome in the fetus. A mongoloid baby has forty-seven chromosomes in its body cells instead of the normal forty-six. It is thought that aging alters the cell-division mechanism so that one pair of chromosomes fails to separate during the formation of an egg cell. Instead of receiving twenty-three chromosomes from the mother, the embryo gets twenty-four, which, when paired with the twenty-three contributed by the sperm, add up to forty-seven. Most mongoloids have three chromosomes in what would normally be a pair of chromosomes identified as Number 21 and the disorder is also called Trisomy 21.

Some medical researchers have theorized that Trisomy 21 can be caused by a defect in sperm production or in the chromosomal arrangement in the embryo right after fertilization. But the most conclusive studies to date show that mongolism is most clearly associated with rising maternal age. The chances of having a mongoloid baby are only one in 2,500 for a mother under twenty. Throughout a woman's twenties they are still very low—about one in 1,500, and for the mother aged thirty to thirty-four they're about one in 850. But for mothers aged thirty-five to thirty-nine they climb to one in 280 and take an even sharper turn upward after a woman reaches forty—to one in 100 between the ages of forty and forty-four and one in 40 after age forty-five.

A similar process can take place in chromosome pairs other than Number 21, and these trisomies, like mongolism, give rise to babies with severe abnormalities. Because a chromosome contains so much genetic information that will govern a baby's development, chromosomal imbalances tend to produce multiple defects involving gross physical deformities and usually some mental retardation. The vast majority of embryos with chromosomal errors do not last long and are the source of many spontaneous abortions during the early weeks of pregnancy. Or, if they survive long enough to be born, they generally die shortly after delivery.

Some of these malformations of chromosomal origin have also been found to be related to the mother's age. Edward's syndrome (Number 18), in which afflicted babies have overlapping digits, low-set ears, rocker-bottom feet, and very low intelligence, and Patau's syndrome (Numbers 13–15), involving babies with too many fingers and toes, congenital heart disease, and a rare form of cleft lip and palate, are more prevalent among children of women over thirty-five. Fortunately, these disorders are exceedingly rare. Trisomy 18 occurs in about one in 4,500 live births, Trisomy 13–15 in only one in 14,500 live births.

Conditions involving extra sex chromosomes, such as XXX and XYY, are not as serious as other types of trisomies. But XYY is thought to encourage deviant behavior and children with a third X chromosome are more likely to suffer from mental retardation or other birth defects. XXX occurs in one out of every 1,700 births, XYY in one out of every 250 to 700 births.

In the abnormality known as Klinefelter's syndrome, advanced paternal age comes into play. This condition, in which a male child has two X chromosomes, is present in one in 400 boys, and is characterized by very small testes which don't produce sperm. Many young men with Klinefelter's syndrome have below-average intelligence as well.

The age of the father appears to be more of a factor in defects where only part of a chromosome is involved. Men over thirty-five run greater risks of fathering children with a type of dwarfism known as achondroplasia, or with a type of deformity in the head, hands, and feet known as acrocephalosyndactyly (Apert syndrome). Advanced paternal age has been found to cause Marfan syndrome. Affected children are exceptionally tall and thin, with heart abnormalities and loosely attached eye lenses.

Children of older fathers are also more likely to have Fibrodysplasia Ossificans Progressiva, in which extra bone develops in the muscles and connective tissue. And recent research has shown paternal age at work in some very rare structural abnormalities.

Other defects caused by older fathers may turn up

in the future. A man's chances of producing a child with a new mutation are thought to increase tenfold between the ages of thirty and sixty. It's for this reason that Dr. Virginia Apgar, director of medical and research programs for the National Foundation–March of Dimes, recommends that "a man should beget his children before he reaches the age of forty-five."

Not all birth defects associated with parental age are genetically caused. An unborn child can also be harmed from some imbalance or malfunction in the environment in which it grows. Older women are more likely to have babies of low birth weight. They may be either premature or "small-for-date," full-term babies who are undersized and weigh less than five and a half pounds. Low-birth-weight infants have a greater chance of dying during the first few years of life or during the birth process itself than those of average size. They are more likely to suffer from brain damage and other neurological problems, including mental retardation.

As maternal age rises, so does the incidence of non-chromosomal cleft lip and palate, congenital heart defects, microcephalus (pinhead), and syndactyly in the baby. Older mothers run an extra risk of having children with spina bifida (incomplete closure of the lower spinal canal) and hydrocephalus (excessive buildup of fluid in the brain). A study of children born in Michigan between 1950 and 1964 shows that an infant's risk of dying from childhood leukemia increases with its mother's age. And women over forty are more prone to have children with cerebral palsy.

Age also affects the capacity of the uterus to sustain a fetus until birth. Compared to a woman aged eighteen, a woman thirty-three or over runs twice the risk of losing a baby before it is born. As both mother and father age, they up the chances for a stillbirth, defined as the death of a fetus twenty-eight weeks old or more.

Women thirty to thirty-four have almost twice as many stillbirths (112 per 1,000 deliveries) as women ten years their junior. The figure trebles after they enter their fourth decade. And the risk of infant mortality is 20 percent higher for women in their late thirties than for women in their twenties, 38 percent higher for women in their forties.

At first glance, this seems like a gloomy picture that is bound to discourage anyone past twenty-nine from even thinking about parenthood. But we have to keep in mind that while these risks to a baby might double or triple with its parents' age, for most abnormalities, they're still very small. Close to 90 percent of the pregnancies with serious chromosomal abnormalities abort spontaneously and only one in 200 births makes it through.

In children of women over thirty, conditions like spina bifida, hydrocephalus, and cleft lip and palate show up only about once in a thousand births. "Clearly, in the absence of a personal history to the contrary," says Dorothy Nortman of the Population Council, "older women run only a small risk of producing a congenitally malformed child, although their risk is much higher than that faced by younger women."

Advances in Preventing Birth Defects

The main exception is Down's syndrome—mongolism—where the risks are considerable to parents in their forties. But now, for this and other congenital disorders, prospective parents in the higher age brackets can reduce the odds against them much further. It has become possible to detect many serious genetic abnormalities and certain other birth defects shortly after conception so that a defective pregnancy can be terminated. The procedure is called amniocentesis, which can be performed after the thirteenth week of pregnancy.

A trained physician inserts a long, hollow needle through a pregnant woman's abdomen and withdraws a sample of amniotic fluid. In the fluid surrounding the fetus in the womb are cells sloughed off by the developing baby. The fluid sample is sent to a laboratory where these fetal cells are cultured and analyzed. Ten to thirty cells are photographed under a microscope as they are dividing. Then the pictures of the cell chromosomes are compared with a normal chromosome arrangement. An irregular chromosome pattern means the fetus has a severe abnormality.

Using this procedure, experts can spot the extra chromosome that causes mongolism, plus the other chromosomal disorders related to advancing parental age. By testing the chemical composition of the amniotic fluid, they can see if the fetus has certain metabolic disorders. With amniocentesis, physicians are able to screen for other genetic defects not related to the parents' age, such as Tay-Sachs disease and hemophilia, plus several severe congenital abnormalities, such as spina bifida. They can also find out if mother and child have an Rh problem or if the fetus isn't receiving enough oxygen. Another bonus of amniocentesis—it tells the baby's sex. Diagnoses with this procedure are 99.5 percent accurate. If the test turns up a serious abnormality, the parents have the choice of bearing the child or aborting it.

Until recently, the procedure was considered somewhat risky. Writings on the matter often turned to the description by Dr. Anonymous in his *Confessions of a Gynecologist:*

> The doctor guides a four-inch needle through the belly wall into the peritoneal cavity, through the uterine wall, and lastly into the amniotic sac. All this must be done without nicking a blood vessel or any of the blood-filled sinuses that are laced around the uterus.

Once you get the needle inside the sac, it mustn't penetrate the fetus itself or any portion of the umbilical cord, which may be looped in any position. You don't push the needle in blindly, however, trusting to luck. You must know how the baby is lying, you locate the placenta so you can avoid it, and you push that needle in with the greatest caution, testing as you go. Still it's a great relief when you get a clear tap—amniotic fluid and no blood.

In addition to puncturing the fetus, amniocentesis that isn't properly administered may cause infection and bleeding in the mother.

In experienced hands, however, amniocentesis is highly accurate and very safe. "Ultrasound"—sound waves of high frequency and low intensity that are far above the range of human hearing—can be beamed toward the fetus inside the mother's abdomen. When they hit something they bounce back and are recorded on an oscilloscope screen, producing a sonogram. The physician is able to use this information to avoid the fetus when inserting the needle. Under these conditions there is less than a 1 percent chance of harm.

From the patient's point of view, the main difficulty appears to be the long wait for the results. To culture and analyze the fetal cells from the amniotic fluid takes from two to five weeks. "The two weeks' waiting for the results were the hardest part of the whole experience," wrote one forty-year-old mother. "I tried to prepare myself should the news be bad. I imagined the abortion and the emptiness afterward." But in the overwhelming majority of cases, the news is good and brings immense relief.

For older parents, amniocentesis is a godsend. With this procedure, as social policy expert Amitai Etzioni points out:

Doctors can tell you with a very high degree of accuracy whether a *particular* fetus is apparently normal or grossly defective. Parents now can literally choose between a mongoloid child and a normal one, and know that if they abort an afflicted fetus, they can very likely replace it with a normal child! It is like the difference between having to go for the jackpot each time, with life at hard labor if you fail, as compared to putting your money on a horse in a race in which there are only two horses in the running, after having been told, with 99 per cent accuracy, which is to be the winner!

But before everyone rushes out for the test, they should know that it isn't a perfect family-planning tool. Amniocentesis can detect the major chromosomal abnormalities and about seventy inherited biochemical disorders, including those caused by age. But it can't predict genetic mutations or screen out every kind of birth defect that exists. And its safety and accuracy depend on the expertise of whoever gives it. Amniocentesis can and is performed in obstetricians' offices, but it is most safe and effective when administered by an obstetrician-geneticist team in a center where it is done often. There the patient can get adequate genetic and psychological counseling and have access to the most sophisticated safety equipment. These centers also maintain stricter quality controls over the laboratories that analyze the amniotic fluid cells than do commercial labs used by individual physicians.

The test is time-consuming and expensive. It costs between $200 and $300 and patients must wait up to five weeks before the results are in. Since amniocentesis is usually performed between the fourteenth and sixteenth weeks of pregnancy, a woman may not find out she is carrying a defective fetus until she is nearly twenty weeks along. If she wants to abort it, the most simple and safe procedures—vacuum suction or dilatation and curettage—used for early pregnancies, are ruled out. She must either have a saline injection, which makes the uterus expel the fetus with laborlike contractions, or, after twenty weeks, a hysterotomy, considered major surgery, in which the fetus is removed from the uterus through a small abdominal incision.

Second-trimester abortions involve a stay in the hospital, and for some people, the decision to abort a fetus that has been found defective can be traumatic. Dr. Kurt Hirschhorn, head of the Division of Human Genetics at Mount Sinai Hospital, found a number of couples in this situation who developed serious psychological problems. Second-trimester abortions are also difficult to obtain in states such as Wisconsin which outlaw therapeutic abortions after the twentieth week of pregnancy. This, in turn, can affect whether amniocentesis is available for prenatal diagnosis of genetic problems at all. In the St. Paul-Minneapolis area, for example, amniocentesis is rarely used to screen for genetic abnormalities because of Catholic pressure against late abortion.

According to the National Foundation–March of Dimes, there were 141 hospital-based centers performing amniocentesis as of 1975. And while their number has shot up since 1968, they're still way too few to meet the current demand. Various centers use different criteria for evaluating their high-priority cases. Some will not recommend routine prenatal testing for mongolism unless a woman is at least forty; others, if she is over thirty-five. A few clinics have set the lower limit for amniocentesis somewhere under thirty-five but over thirty. "Ideally, I think women aged thirty-five or over should have amniocentesis, but here we draw the line at thirty-seven," says Dr. Desider Rothe, who heads the high-risk maternity clinic at New York Hospital–Cornell Medical Center.

Much depends on the judgment of the doctor. One physician in charge of a genetic counseling clinic did not routinely inform his patients over forty about the availability of amniocentesis to avoid stirring up false worries. One sociological study found that only two thirds of the two hundred board-certified gynecologists who answered a questionnaire sent to five hundred in the profession told their older patients about this procedure.

As time goes on, we can expect many of these difficulties to be ironed out. Facilities for amniocentesis continue to multiply and should be widely available in areas not hostile to late abortions within the next five to ten years. As the procedure is perfected, more doctors will recommend its use and more patients will ask to have it done.

Some medical experts have recommended that amniocentesis become a routine part of prenatal care for all pregnancies. Others have reservations. "Even with ultrasound," says Dr. Sheldon H. Cherry of Mount Sinai Hospital, who pioneered in using amniocentesis for fetal research, "it's not a benign procedure." Dr. Cherry routinely recommends amniocentesis to women in their late thirties and older. For women between thirty-five and thirty-seven, it's elective. They're in a borderline age range where the genetic risks are much higher than for women in their twenties but considerably lower than for women over forty. In these cases Dr. Cherry explains to his patients the relative risks of having amniocentesis weighed against the chances for an abnormal baby. Dr. Cherry discourages women in their early thirties from using the procedure. "For them," he says, "it's not worth the risk."

Unless you're forty or over, deciding about amniocentesis can be quite confusing. How can an older couple find out whether or not to use this procedure? The first stop might be the woman's obstetrician. If he or she can't administer amniocentesis or is not interested in using it, the couple could go for another opinion. They might want to consult a specialist associated with a hospital center where amniocentesis is frequently performed. Most of these centers are in our major urban areas and can be located through the National Foundation–March of Dimes.

They could also find out how to deal with age-related risks to an unborn child from a genetic counselor. A genetic counselor is a professional trained to dispense advice on preventing or handling hereditary disorders. By taking a family history and giving various tests, the counselor can tell prospective parents precisely what their children's chances of having certain genetic abnormalities are. The counseling process also involves helping the couple decide how to deal with genetic risks— whether to take the chance of having a baby, to abort it, or to refrain from having children altogether. Besides finding out how to handle age-related disorders, a visit to a genetic counselor can be helpful in determining the child's chances of having other types of defects, such as hemophilia or sickle-cell anemia, which aren't caused by the parents' age.

Many prominent medical authorities routinely recommend genetic counseling for women over forty— and in some cases, women over thirty-five—who are having their first child. There are hundreds of centers in this country with genetic counseling units. Most are associated with hospitals, medical schools, or research institutions and are concentrated on the East and West Coasts. Some of these centers have facilities for amniocentesis. They can be located in the *International Directory— Birth Defects, Genetic Services* published by the National Foundation–March of Dimes.

What Are the Risks to the Older Mother?

What about the older mother herself? Does she take extra chances, too? To a certain extent, yes. Older women run above-average risks to their own health as well as that of their babies, especially after they reach forty. World Health Organization statistics published in 1969 show that in countries with low maternal mortality, such as the United States and Sweden, women aged forty to forty-four had an average of 248 deaths per 100,000 live births, three times the number for women thirty to thirty-four and nearly nine times the number for women twenty to twenty-four.

But while these figures show older women run proportionately higher risks, their actual risk of death from pregnancy is still low. And it becomes even lower with access to good medical care. The medical profession deals with this problem by putting first-time mothers over thirty-five into a special "high risk" category. Physicians call a woman thirty-five or over who is bearing her first child an "elderly primipara" or "elderly primigravida." The Council of the International Federation of Obstetricians and Gynecologists adopted the age of thirty-five as the cut-off point for defining the elderly primigravida in 1958. The term is used to bring a doctor's attention to the higher level of risk faced by pregnant women above that age so that they will treat them with special care.

The obstetrician handling an elderly primigravida or a woman approaching that age range knows that she has a greater chance of developing complications during pregnancy and delivery than the average patient. He or she will keep a sharp lookout for toxemia, a condition during the last part of pregnancy involving high blood pressure, heavy fluid retention in the tissues, and the presence of protein in a woman's urine. Toxemia can prevent the placenta from functioning properly and, in its serious form, is among the three leading causes of maternal mortality. Women bearing their first child in their late thirties are about twice as likely to develop toxemia as those in their twenties.

The older woman's obstetrician also wants to make sure she hasn't developed placenta previa, which can threaten both mother's and baby's lives. In placenta previa the fertilized egg implants itself too low in the uterus, so that the placenta forms at the lower end of the uterus rather than toward the top, covering part or all of its opening neck. As the uterine opening, or cervix, begins to expand late in pregnancy in preparation for labor, it tears loose any part of the placenta attached to it. This can cause severe bleeding in the mother and deprive the baby of sufficient oxygen and food. In first-time mothers thirty-five and over, placenta previa occurs in 7 out of 100 births, about three and one half times more often than for women under twenty-five.

Chronic conditions that are more common in older women can add to the complications. A woman will find it much more difficult to carry a baby if she has kidney disease or a heart condition. If she has diabetes, she has a greater chance of developing toxemia, or fluid retention, and her child's chances of being stillborn or dying during the first few weeks of life range from 10 to 35 percent. A pregnant woman will easily develop another form of toxemia if she has a history of hypertension or high blood pressure. The obstetrician treating women with any of these problems will watch them closely and may give them special tests or diets.

A vigilant physician will scrutinize women who think they're susceptible to breast cancer, too. Some recent studies have found that women who become pregnant later in life have a higher incidence of this disease. The risk of breast cancer rises with the age a woman has her first child, but it climbs more sharply after she passes the mid-thirties mark.

This is not to say that pregnancy itself is a cause of breast cancer, for it occurs more frequently in women who have never had children than in women having their first baby under thirty-five. We still don't know enough about breast cancer to pinpoint its cause, and I don't think the danger of breast cancer warrants having one's family early. But if you believe your risk of breast cancer is above average to begin with, you should discuss your plans for delaying pregnancy with your doctor.

What about labor and delivery? Studies of the obstetrical performances of older women show that they run into more problems. One by Sidney Kane on more than 36,000 women aged twenty-five or over who were pregnant for the first time indicated abnormal fetal presentation among 31 percent of the women aged forty to forty-four and 24 percent of those thirty-five to thirty-nine, compared to 18 percent of the women twenty-five to twenty-nine. Postpartum hemorrhage from uterine inertia, or weak contractions, was 6.2 percent and 2.7 percent in the older versus younger age groups. Other investigations of first pregnancies in older women found that 30 percent of the elderly primigravida had labors that required the use of forceps (compared to 10 percent of women under twenty-five); and between 25 and 31 percent needed Caesarean sections (compared to 10 to 15 percent of all births).

Most obstetrical textbooks tell us that older women will have to spend as much as 25 percent more time in labor. But whether this means a really prolonged and difficult labor is a point of debate. The late Dr. Alan Guttmacher, one of the nation's leading authorities on obstetrics and gynecology, wrote:

Almost all observers agree that a first pregnancy after the age of thirty-five, when women are classed as elderly primiparas, is attended by an increase in the length of labor. Today we believe that the difficulty is due to the replacement of some of the easily stretched elastic tissue cells and muscle connective tissue cells.

Even though women are still young at thirty-five, from the standpoint of childbearing their span is more than two-thirds over.

Clinical professor of obstetrics and gynecology at New York Hospital–Cornell Medical Center Dr. William J. Sweeney III compared the older first-time mother to "a boxer over the hill. Her muscle tone is not good enough, neither is her endurance. She knows the words, but she can't play the tune." But Dr. Cherry takes issue. "There's no earthly reason," he told me, "why a normal woman aged thirty-seven should have a more difficult labor than a normal woman aged twenty-five."

Most of the older women I interviewed did not have troublesome labors. Several had remarkably easy deliveries. One forty-one-year-old had a near-painless delivery. "I woke up and the contractions were coming two minutes apart," she said. "By the time we got to the hospital I was ready for delivery and they didn't have time to prepare me. I didn't even have to use my Lamaze breathing and hardly had to push at all! There was only one point when I felt some discomfort. I said to myself, 'If this keeps up, it could get tricky.' What I didn't know at the time was that I was in transition (the most difficult part of labor) and it was all about over."

One thirty-nine-year-old whose obstetrician had miscalculated her due date was thrown off guard when labor started five weeks before schedule. "I had counted on using some form of pain relief," she recalled. "But when I got to the labor room they told me I was soon going into delivery and didn't need it. Oh, I did some groaning, but it didn't last long. It was lucky my doctor lived near the hospital or he wouldn't have made it."

Several women reported complications. Two went through forty-eight hours of "false labor"—irregular uterine contractions that don't dilate the cervix—that later turned into the real thing. Their obstetricians had to use forceps to complete their deliveries. I encountered only two women who had to have Caesarean sections. Both were very small and narrowly built. One had a poor health record—part of a lung removed, fibroid tumors, multiple miscarriages, and her pregnancy had been predictably difficult.

The overwhelming majority of the older women I interviewed worked or kept up their normal activities until the day their babies were born. Most had found their nine months of waiting exhilarating but uneventful. These were typical responses: "It was the healthiest and one of the most marvelous times in my life." "I had a great pregnancy, a very easy one. I played better tennis than I ever had before or have since."

I found no pattern among the older women I interviewed that distinguished their childbirth experiences from those of women much younger. What stood out was their attitude toward having a baby. These women all appeared to have gone through pregnancy with a remarkable degree of composure, even the ones who ran into trouble. In their descriptions of pregnancy, labor, and delivery, I didn't discern a single note of hysteria or complaint.

I wouldn't want to call the group I interviewed a representative sample of older mothers, for mine was not meant to be a laboratory study. Statistically, older women do have longer labors and more problem-filled pregnancies with their first births; there are more than enough studies to document this. But we should keep in mind that the statistics on maternal complications are statistics, not people. A woman's capacity to go through pregnancy and delivery depends a great deal on her individual physical and mental makeup. A healthy woman close to forty, in good shape, with no history of chronic disease, may perform as well as one ten to fifteen years younger. According to Dr. Arthur Davids of Manhattan, "The American woman is not old at forty. Physically she can pass for thirty if she's well nourished and has good medical care . . . Kidney disease, hypertension, diabetes, cardiac disease, these have to be ruled out, but younger women can get them, too."

Moreover, the level of risk to a woman at any age depends on her socio-economic background. Women from middle- or upper-middle-class backgrounds will generally have fewer obstetrical complications of all sorts than those from the lower class. Poorer women are less likely to have the means to keep themselves properly nourished and in good health, or to get good prenatal care.

States Dorothy Nortman of the Population Council, "The tremendous variation in space and time and across different social classes is strong testimony that social and economic factors have a great deal to do with the absolute levels of risk at any age . . . Because of these exogenous factors, while the relative risk with age seems to persist across different classes, there is a wide variance in the absolute level of risk . . . the socio-economic background of the parents is the chief determinant of the level of risk."

A woman pushing forty who is well informed about her body, who understands her needs during pregnancy, and who gets proper medical attention may have a much better chance in pregnancy and childbirth than a disadvantaged woman many years her junior. According to Dr. Rothe, "Older women aren't that statistically different. I really don't think being older makes such a big difference. What is more important is the individual, her education and attitude. Women over forty who are educated and well prepared do better than the young twenty-one-year-old who is not well educated and comes in screaming. If you check the hospital charts, statistically, the complications in poor people who are young are much higher than for our older patients. I think the attitude is so important."

Some medical researchers and practicing obstetricians even feel there is no more reason to tag a woman of thirty-five as "high risk" than one who is thirty. "There would appear to be no evidence whatsoever for picking the arbitrary age of thirty-five years for the flashing of a danger signal," says Sidney Kane. "The concept of the arbitrary age [thirty-five years] at which maternal risk increases should be abandoned as a myth and the more logical concept of a sliding scale of difficulty should replace it."

There's nothing qualitatively different about a pregnancy after age thirty-five. An elderly primigravida may have a higher level of risk to herself and her baby. But the risks are from the same kinds of complications faced by younger women—it's just that we expect them to occur more often. And what an older first-time mother needs is not a special type of treatment for pregnant crones but high-quality medical care—a physician and hospital facilities that can handle, and have had experience with, the whole run of complications associated with having a baby.

Finding the Right Medical Care

This country may not have the lowest infant or maternal mortality rates on the globe or medical care that is free and equal for all, but it still ranks among the group of nations that lead the world in the management of childbirth. For those who have the knowledge and financial means, it can deliver a high level of medical care. Most pregnancies of older women will be normal in any event. However, suppose you're over thirty-five, feel fine, but want to take every precaution. Or you're younger but fear you might run into complications. What steps should you take to insure that your pregnancy will be a success?

First of all, a couple should plan for pregnancy long before conception. Because an unborn baby's growth is totally dependent on the mother's body, it's important for the mother to maintain good health. "Ideally, the kind of medical care that helps a woman provide a healthy, nourishing environment for her unborn child," says Dr. Virginia Apgar, "begins long before pregnancy, even as early as the mother's own prenatal life. It should continue throughout her own growing-up years so that she will begin motherhood in optimum good health." This advice applies to women of all ages, but should be heeded even more carefully by women who want to minimize the effect of age on their reproductive capacity.

No matter what a woman's age, most medical authorities recommend that she see a physician before becoming pregnant. "Every woman," says Dr. Sheldon Cherry, "should have a good physical examination and a complete checkup to make sure she has no pelvic infections or other medical problems." By consulting a doctor before conception, a woman can find out if she has any abnormalities, such as diabetes or high blood pressure, that could complicate a pregnancy. She can get some inkling of possible fertility problems or information on drugs or habits—such as smoking—that could interfere with conception or normal fetal growth.

A preliminary visit to the doctor is also an opportunity to check out immunity to German measles. Here, advance planning is a must. If a woman needs anti-rubella vaccine, she has to wait at least several months after vaccination before trying to conceive. Older couples can use their pre-pregnancy visit to ask about genetic counseling or the husband's fertility status.

If an older couple has been cleared for childbearing, the next step is to find appropriate medical care during pregnancy and delivery. Today a range of maternity services is available in many areas. A couple may select from a number of different methods of supervising pregnancy and from various settings for delivery. They can have their baby in the hospital, at home, or in an outpatient maternity facility, with or without anesthesia or episiotomy, delivered by a physician, nurse-midwife, or experienced friend. Each style of childbirth has its set of champions and critics, and the most suitable forms of maternity care depend a great deal on a couple's medical profile and personal taste. Which are best for older parents?

Home delivery may be the most warm and personal way to welcome a baby into the family, and is becoming something of a trend in California and some urban areas. But it makes physicians see red. Dr. Landrum B. Shettles, in a letter to *The New York Times*, summarized the position of the medical profession:

> The decrease in infant and maternal morbidity and mortality in modern times reflects not only good prenatal and newborn care but also births being carried out with ample facilities in readiness for any unforeseen emergency during labor and delivery or immediately thereafter. Fetal distress for various reasons, prolapsed umbilical cords, hemorrhage, infection are grave problems in the best-equipped surroundings, let alone in the home with little or no help. The important point to remember is that today the very same unsuspected emergencies can arise as in the days when an infant and/ or expectant mother was cited as "lost in childbirth." . . . Valuable time lost in transit after an emergency has arisen in the home or even after arrival in an emergency hospital facility might otherwise have proved to be lifesaving. Consequently, to maintain the greatest overall safety in maternity practice, we do not approve of home deliveries. Neither has the American College

of Obstetricians nor the American Academy of Pediatrics given their sanction for births electively at home. A single loss of a baby or mother under such inadequate circumstances is simply unacceptable.

Whether or not one accepts this view, only the most normal and easy deliveries should be carried out at home. And as Dr. Thomas P. Kerenyi, director of Mount Sinai Hospital's perinatology division, points out, "The biggest problem is how to identify the high-risk population. There is no foolproof method for prediction. Some high-risk women, such as diabetics, you know about ahead of time, but you can find young women in the ideal reproductive age group, perfectly healthy, thinking very positively about pregnancy and childbirth, who develop problems there was no way to anticipate, not only during labor but in the delivery room right in the middle of birth." It has been estimated that about 40 percent of all complications that arise during birth can't be identified in advance.

If an older couple is set against standard obstetrical care, they may—in certain cases—be able to work with a nurse-midwife connected with a hospital. Trained nurse-midwives working closely with their patients throughout pregnancy and delivery offer more individual attention and psychological support than standard obstetrical services. They generally cost much less than obstetricians. In the event of complications the nurse-midwife is always backed up by an obstetrician. Such midwife programs are designed to handle normal pregnancies and labors and are approved "in medically directed teams" for "uncomplicated maternity patients" by the American College of Obstetricians and Gynecologists.

For the older couple, using this form of maternity care successfully depends on their age, physical condition, and the facilities surrounding the midwife program. At New York's Roosevelt Hospital, emergency services and equipment for the nurse-midwives are immediately on tap. But the program at the Maternity Center Association's Childbearing Center in Manhattan is in a former private home and has come under fire for being eleven minutes from its back-up hospital. The Childbearing Center will accept only low-risk candidates and women who are having their first child at age thirty-five and under. Roosevelt's nurse-midwife service, on the other hand, does not set an arbitrary age limit on its patients. It examines each prospective case thoroughly and will take women with uncomplicated pregnancies in their thirties. But few women over thirty-five have used this facility.

One writer specializing in health problems likened having a physician supervise pregnancy and birth to fire insurance. "Most of the time," he said, "it doesn't matter what kind of fire insurance you have or even if you have it. It doesn't matter, that is, unless you have a fire. Then you need insurance in the worst way, and you want and need the very best kind. Similarly, as happened for thousands of years, the vast majority of births would turn out perfectly well without a physician or a hospital. The only justification for either is as insurance against the unusual or unexpected."

Most women over thirty-five are destined to have completely uneventful pregnancies. If, however, they already have a spotty health record, they should give their choice of obstetrician and hospital facilities serious thought. These are some of the medical conditions most obstetricians consider high-risk:

MOTHER'S AGE
Under 16
Over 40

BIRTH NUMBER
First child to woman thirty-five or older

RH FACTOR
Rh incompatibility when the wife is Rh negative and the husband is Rh positive

MOTHER'S HEALTH PROBLEMS
Anemia
Heart, circulatory, or kidney disease; high blood pressure
Diabetes
Malnutrition or obesity
Urinary tract infection
Rubella infection of mother during pregnancy (sometimes requires therapeutic abortion but can be prevented by vaccination before pregnancy)
Emotional instability
Tuberculosis
Syphilis or gonorrhea
Toxoplasmosis (an infection carried by animals, especially cats, but most frequently contracted by eating rare meat)

ANATOMICAL DEFECTS
Android (manlike) pelvis
Incompetent cervix (where the mouth of the uterus doesn't remain closed enough to hold the developing fetus)

GENETIC PROBLEMS
Relatives or ancestors with genetic defects such as Down's syndrome or Tay-Sachs disease

OTHER HIGH-RISK CATEGORIES
Drug addicts, heavy smokers, heavy drinkers
The unwed, separated, or divorced
The poverty-stricken
Anyone under unusual stress

If you have to add any other risk factor to your age, you should consider using an obstetrician and a hospital equipped to handle complicated cases. This type of care is generally available in our urban areas where there are hospitals with large and well-staffed obstetrical divisions. Particularly well suited for complicated cases are teaching hospitals associated with medical schools, and hospitals with perinatal centers—special units which provide intensive care for high-risk pregnancies and high-risk infants.

As Dr. Karlis Adamsons of Mount Sinai Hospital points out, "A doctor who delivers two hundred babies a year has only about 5 percent complicated cases, or ten per year. That's not much experience. Whereas, if a doctor is in charge of a university hospital, or any hospital delivering two thousand to ten thousand patients, he develops a totally different degree of expertise." This type of facility is also more likely to have access to amniocentesis and other procedures for dealing with problems.

If possible, a couple should select their obstetrician and medical facility while they are still planning the pregnancy. In many cases the older woman's regular obstetrician-gynecologist will do nicely. But if she needs someone with more background in obstetrics or experience with complications, she might want to do some shopping around.

Sometimes the right kind of doctor can be found by word of mouth, especially from other older parents. Or you can call a nearby medical school or medical-school-affiliated hospital, ask for the obstetrics department, and obtain a list of department members with private practices. They are most likely to have the strongest professional credentials and the most up-to-date knowledge in their field. An obstetrician affiliated with a hospital that has a strong obstetrics wing is also a good bet. The county medical society or local Planned Parenthood chapter is another source of names of licensed obstetricians and gynecologists.

In many cities women's health collectives and counseling services do careful referrals. For example, the National Women's Health Coalition keeps evaluations of the professional competence of physicians and clinics and will even try to match their recommendations to each woman's needs. It plans to publish a directory of recommended physicians in all specialties, hospitals, and clinics. Local offices of the National Organization for Women (NOW) keep track of nearby counseling services. The Health Research Group, 2000 P Street N.W., Washington, D.C. 20036, also has a list of directories of physicians for certain areas.

After obtaining the names of some recommended obstetricians, you may want to learn more about them before making an appointment. Information on an obstetrician's training, experience, and certification credentials can be found in the *American Medical Directory* and the *Directory of Medical Specialists,* which are found in all medical libraries, county medical societies, and many public libraries. You can find out if an obstetrician is board-certified by writing to the American College of Obstetricians and Gynecologists, 1 Wacker Drive, Chicago, Illinois.

It's probably wise to avoid doctors without any hospital affiliation or ones associated only with small private profit-making hospitals, which are generally not equipped to handle severe complications. Many medical experts believe that any type of hospital handling less than five hundred deliveries—and in some cases one thousand deliveries—a year won't usually have the necessary complement of trained personnel and emergency equipment for complications. The hospital should be accredited by the Joint Committee on Accreditation of Hospitals, 645 N. Michigan Avenue, Chicago, Illinois 60611; one third of all American hospitals aren't.

It may also be an advantage to choose a physician who works in a team with one or two others. Doctors in these group practices are inclined to screen each other carefully and to consult with their partners in complicated cases. For an obstetrical patient, especially one going into labor, there's a special advantage: if her regular doctor is away or delivering someone else, she can be cared for by one of the partners, as opposed to a hospital resident or a doctor new to her case.

And before making a final decision, a couple preparing for pregnancy should be sure they are satisfied with their selection of a doctor. It's especially important that an older woman find someone who is not only thorough but willing to take the time to deal with any fears about complications or other special needs she might have.

Of course, this kind of specialized care will cost more than the midwife services or a general practitioner. Older parents, however, are more likely to have the means to pay for it. If you have reason to believe you'll run into a barrage of complications, you should consider adding to your health insurance. Most policies won't pay enough to cover even a normal delivery, and many don't include the first two weeks or month of hospital care for newborns with difficulties. Only a few have begun to subsidize amniocentesis.

Several weeks of hospitalization for an infant or mother with complications can run into the thousands. You should look into a separate comprehensive major medical policy available through your employer or insurance agent or a prepaid health plan, such as Kaiser-Permanente in California or HIP (Health Insurance Plan) in New York City, to cover any problem during pregnancy or the first few weeks of the baby's life. To find out more about these plans or others in your area, you can write to the Group Health Association of America, Inc., 2121 Pennsylvania Avenue N.W., Washington, D.C. 20005, and the Health Insurance Association of America, 750 Third Avenue, New York, N.Y. 10017.

Another possibility for couples who can't afford private physicians or heavy insurance payments—but still need high-quality maternity care—is the maternity clinic of a teaching hospital. There a woman will be treated by the obstetrical residents on the staff and her baby will be delivered by whoever is on call at the time. Usually she will have to pay only for her hospital room. She may not get the personal attention she would from a private doctor, but she has the advantage of working with trained specialists in a hospital with the most up-to-date facilities. The staff and services of maternity clinics run by public hospitals are generally not as good.

How Is a Late Pregnancy Handled?

Once an obstetrician has been selected, is there anything different about the way he or she will handle an older woman's pregnancy? If the patient is in her late thirties, she may be encouraged to have amniocentesis or to see a genetic counselor. Some doctors will want to examine her more frequently than their younger patients as she nears term. And they will be constantly on the watch for complications. Unless serious difficulties are immediately apparent, the physical side of her pregnancy will be handled pretty much the same as for women in their twenties, with just an extra dose of caution.

Special attention may need to be paid, however, to the older woman's psychological needs. In all women, the physical changes of pregnancy set off profound emotional reactions. "It seems universally true that women experience pregnancy as a psychological crisis," state psychologists Arthur and Libby Coleman. "It could not be otherwise. Shifts in body image, secretions of hormones and the maze of changing environmental supports and cultural expectations are inevitably mirrored in the psyche, in the mental life of the pregnant woman."

Pregnant women are more susceptible to sharp swings of feeling and rapidly shifting moods, a state called "emotional lability." Often their emotional vulnerability gives rise to fears—worries about the safety of the unborn child and the effect of a baby on the couple's lifestyle. An older woman in particular is apt to have intense fears about having a deformed baby. Explains obstetrician E. A. J. Alment:

> Whilst she is likely to be better informed about pregnancy and its complications than her younger counterpart, her awareness can deprive her of the protection of blissful ignorance which is part of the inborn optimism of the young primigravida. Fear of foetal malformation is one of the primary concerns of pregnant women, and this is especially true of the elderly primigravida. Her encounter in a large antenatal clinic with a vast majority of young patients, many of them multiparous, can give her a sense of inadequacy, of late arrival, and make her withdrawn and sensitive, and less able to communicate her problems.

Since the chances of an older woman actually bearing a deformed baby are so small, and totally disproportionate to her level of anxiety, it is up to her physician to put such fears into perspective. Obstetricians who handle older pregnancies expect to spend more time giving their patients reassurance. "I have to give my older patients more emotional support," says Dr. Rothe. "They're much more afraid of having an abnormal baby and they require more time and attention." On the other hand, making too much of an older mother's special needs can backfire and may still make her feel self-conscious. "I don't think these older patients should be singled out and made to feel different," Dr. Rothe adds.

A woman can do a great deal to prevent complications herself by seeing her obstetrician regularly and following his or her suggestions for prenatal care. It has been estimated that if all women had good prenatal care, two thirds of the complications of pregnancy could be detected and treated. One aspect of sound prenatal care that is currently getting more emphasis is proper nutrition. During pregnancy an older woman might want to pay particular attention to what she eats. Some recent studies have shown that the popular belief that the fetus will take what it needs from the mother's body does not hold. Many babies whose mothers did not eat sufficient amounts of the right nutrients were found to be underweight and even brain-damaged. Malnutrition aggravates conditions such as toxemia in late pregnancy that are more common in older mothers.

Growing numbers of doctors have now abandoned the old rigid laws that set arbitrary limits, such as sixteen to twenty pounds, on a woman's weight gain during pregnancy. They're checking not only the number of pounds a woman gains but how they are put on. The pattern of weight gain is important. And what makes up those extra pounds also counts—recommended diets for pregnancy usually call for increased protein intake. Dr. John C. Hobbins, assistant professor of obstetrics and gynecology and of diagnostic radiology, and director of the high-risk program at the Yale-New Haven Hospital, even suggests that a woman who plans to become pregnant watch what she eats, especially the amount of protein, for at least a year before she tries to conceive. "During that time," he notes, "she can make up most of the nutritional deficits she may have incurred earlier."

The National Foundation–March of Dimes has a pamphlet on nutrition prepared in cooperation with the Institute of Human Nutrition at Columbia University College of Physicians and Surgeons that explains the importance of proper diet during pregnancy. It can be obtained by writing to the National Foundation–March of

Dimes. There are good discussions of nutrition during pregnancy and other aspects of prenatal care in Dr. Sheldon H. Cherry's *Understanding Pregnancy and Childbirth* and the late Dr. Alan Guttmacher's *Pregnancy, Birth and Family Planning*. For the supercautious or health-food fans who want an even more detailed nutritional guide, Adelle Davis has written *Let's Have Healthy Children*.

Besides watching what she eats, a pregnant woman should be careful of what she smokes. Babies of smoking mothers have nearly four times the level of carbon monoxide in their blood as those of non-smokers. Smoking tends to retard fetal development and smokers often have babies that are smaller than average. Some studies have found that smoking can cause miscarriage, stillbirth, and newborn death. Harmful to the baby, too, are X rays and certain drugs. All women should discuss their food and drug intake carefully with their obstetrician. If age cuts down on reproductive efficiency, the proper approach to diet and drugs can help counteract this.

As part of prenatal care, obstetrics has worked out methods for diagnosing toxemia or treating complications from diabetes or a heart condition. Through frequent testing of blood, blood pressure, and urine, these problems can be closely watched throughout pregnancy. Doctors now prescribe special diets and physical regimens to keep these conditions under control or drugs that prevent the buildup of excess body fluids. Women can also help reduce these and other serious problems by learning how to spot potential complications themselves. Most of the current guides to pregnancy and childbirth detail various warning signals. Being well informed goes a long way toward minimizing childbirth risks.

On the whole, the way medicine handles a woman's pregnancy has become more sophisticated. Recent advances in obstetrics, gynecology, and pediatrics have included successful methods of treatment for even the most high-risk cases. There have evolved intricate sub-specialties, such as fetology (study and care of the fetus) and neonatology (study and care of the newborn) to deal with complications before and after birth. Our major hospitals have special perinatal centers staffed by geneticists, embryologists, fetologists, neonatologists, pediatricians, surgeons, endocrinologists, pediatric nurses, and psychiatric social workers to handle childbearing problems throughout pregnancy and the first month of the baby's life. Some of these centers register rates of fetal, maternal, and infant illness and mortality for high-risk pregnancies that are below the national average for all births.

At maternity clinics in these centers, or in the hands of a competent obstetrician, many of the complications of high-risk pregnancies—including those related to age—can be detected and eliminated. An older couple can receive genetic counseling and advice on appropriate prenatal care. From the third month of pregnancy on, a physician can use ultrasound, not only for amniocentesis, but also to determine the size and position of the fetus and placenta and to chart the baby's growth. Ultrasound also helps detect multiple pregnancies (which are more common in older women), hydrocephaly and anenceph-aly, hydramnion (excess amniotic fluid), myomas (mus-cular tumors), and ovarian cysts.

In addition to diagnosing birth defects, amniocente-sis is used during the last three months of pregnancy to see if the baby is being endangered by Rh blood disease, diabetes, or toxemia. Chemical analysis of the amniotic fluid can measure the age of the fetus to see if the baby is mature enough to survive if an early delivery is required. Another way obstetricians observe the condition of the baby before birth is with a lighted endoscope inserted into the vagina. This device rests on the membrane of the cervix and through it the color of the amniotic fluid can be seen. Yellow-green fluid is a sign of fetal distress, usually from oxygen deprivation, and indicates the need for an early delivery. New procedures are being investigated in fetal medicine and fetal surgery. In the future it may be possible to give medicine to, and even operate on, a baby while it is still in the womb.

Labor and Delivery: The Options for Older Parents

One of the most dangerous times in a baby's life is during the birth process. Difficulties during labor can lead to permanent brain damage or even the loss of the baby's life. Some of the recent obstetrical developments make labor and delivery much safer. Doctors can now measure the size of a baby's head to see if the mother's pelvis is wide enough for a natural delivery. If there are signs that the baby isn't getting enough oxygen, the physician can measure the oxygen content from a sample drawn from the scalp. It is even possible to make an electroencephalogram of the baby's brain activity during birth.

Perhaps the most widely hailed advance against damage from birth is the electronic fetal monitor, which continuously records the baby's heartbeat during labor. An external monitor is fastened around the mother's abdomen to measure uterine contractions and the baby's heartbeat. An internal monitor operates through thin wires inserted up the birth canal and attached to the exposed part of the baby's scalp. By observing the pattern of the baby's pulse in relation to labor contractions, doctors can tell if the baby is receiving enough oxygen.

If the monitor or fetal blood sample shows signs of trouble, the doctor will try to reposition the mother or administer oxygen or intravenous fluids. An emergency Caesarean section will be performed as a last resort. However, the monitor also prevents unnecessary Caesareans by showing whether the other means helping the baby are effective. And fetal monitoring can help doctors regulate the amount of medication and pain-relieving drugs administered to the mother, since these may add to the chances of fetal asphyxiation.

A woman's age may influence the way a problem labor is handled. The obstetrician treating an elderly primigravida is likely to operate under the assumption that "her first pregnancy may be her last." States Dr. Sheldon Cherry: "The elderly primipara concept in obstetrics has been ill-defined. What it means to me is that a woman having a baby in her late thirties or early forties has less of a chance of having another pregnancy. Obstetrics will put a higher premium on the fetus and infant in relation to the risks to the mother." In other words, the physician will tend to intervene more actively on behalf of the baby in an older woman's labor and delivery. For complications such as membranes that rupture before the onset of labor or prolonged labor, he or she will be more conservative with an older patient than with the one in her twenties. Instead of waiting to see if the older woman works up to a healthy labor, the doctor might perform a Caesarean section earlier.

But bracing for complications doesn't mean an older couple should overreact. Even when the woman is over forty, there's less reason to expect a difficult delivery or Caesarean section than a completely normal one. If this is so, can older couples plan for natural or prepared childbirth? Will the mother be able to go through labor and delivery without anesthesia like younger women?

Many features of prepared childbirth are especially well suited to a mature and knowledgeable couple. Men and women planning to use this method attend a series of prenatal classes, which teach a repertoire of breathing and relaxation exercises designed to minimize pain. The classes discuss in detail all aspects of the birth process to dispel common fears and misinformation that can make childbirth overly traumatic. During labor the couple works together as a team so that both husband and wife share in their child's birth. Fathers are usually allowed into the delivery room.

Prepared childbirth thus involves more than simple pain relief. It lets the father play an important part in the birth of his child that can set the pattern for his role in family life. And, as childbirth education authority Constance Bean points out, "Learning about childbirth offers the opportunity to prepare for a new life experience with the additional opportunity to learn to understand and respect the functioning of the body."

Women trained in childbirth skills generally need less medication during labor, and often none at all. But the typical childbirth-education class is slanted toward the normal uncomplicated delivery. It leaves the medical problems that can crop up during labor to the obstetrician. The aim, of course, is to downplay accumulated negative attitudes toward birth and unnecessary fears. This makes sense when 95 percent of all births are reported normal. But how does it work for the older couple, who can expect a higher incidence of complications?

Raquel Trost, childbirth-education instructor at Mount Sinai Hospital in New York, feels that there is a "unique positive dimension" to the motivation of the mature couple who expect their first child during their thirties. "I know this goes against what is written in all the textbooks on obstetrics," she says, "but in my experience, the older women generally have easier labors and need less medication. I have seen, among older women, very few cases where a Caesarean was called for."

In Mrs. Trost's view, older couples make good candidates for prepared childbirth. "A couple in their thirties," she observed, "know what they want, and when they have a baby, it is a more free and responsible choice." Mrs. Trost thinks that younger couples are more likely to go for prepared childbirth "because it is the thing to do." The older couple, on the other hand, she finds less pressured, and when they opt for prepared childbirth, it is because they have made an informed and conscious decision. When older women run into problems that require some anesthetic, they tend to react with less of a sense of failure or disappointment.

Childbirth-education experts generally believe that even complicated deliveries are handled better with childbirth training. The prepared woman, as Constance Bean argues, "can respond to directives, avoid panic, and accept intervention such as anesthesia and forceps when these are required." "Even people that had problems say that their training helped," says Mrs. Trost. "They say they couldn't have waited the hours they did before, for example, a Caesarean was finally performed." Women who were told they had to have Caesareans in advance have said that prepared-childbirth techniques helped them cope with daily discomfort during the last stages of pregnancy.

Obviously, older couples should not feel they have to rule out prepared childbirth. "I encourage everyone to use Lamaze," says Dr. Rothe. And generally being more well informed about childbirth than their younger colleagues, late parents may even get more enjoyment and satisfaction from childbirth training. In one prepared-childbirth class at Mount Sinai I observed, it was the older couple who had the most intelligent and penetrating questions.

If prepared-childbirth training does not give enough pain relief, or if an older woman runs into complications requiring medication, recent breakthroughs in obstetrical anesthesia make her delivery safer and more pleasant. In the past few decades most women went into the delivery room unconscious. They received general anesthesia, either inhaling a mixture of nitrous oxide and oxygen gases or receiving an injection of sodium pentothal. During labor they got pain-relieving analgesics such as Demerol and, frequently, scopolamine—the "truth serum" of World War II spy thrillers that erases memory of pain but causes wild, uncontrollable behavior.

But these medications had serious drawbacks. Most passed across the placenta into the baby's bloodstream. Heavy doses of analgesics, in combination with general anesthesia, often produced overly sleepy babies with delayed weight gain and sucking response and, once in a while, inhibited respiration. The mother would emerge from delivery weak and dizzy, ill equipped to begin caring for her child. Her role in giving birth was passive, often assisted by forceps. This prolonged her labor, with some threat to the baby's well-being, and the mother did not see her child being born. There was also the danger of vomiting while under general anesthesia. Food thereby breathed into the lungs could cause pneumonia and was the greatest source of maternal deaths in this country.

Some of these problems have been solved by conduction anesthesia, which doesn't blot out consciousness but only blocks conduction of pain sensations to the brain. It eliminates pain from a specific region of the body; thus, the mother can remain awake throughout delivery. Relatively little is absorbed into the mother's bloodstream or crosses the placenta, so babies delivered with conduction anesthesia are generally quite awake. Most forms of the medication can be used for pain relief in labor as well as delivery.

The three major forms of conduction anesthesia are spinal, epidural, and caudal. With spinal anesthesia the drug is injected into the spinal canal to eliminate pain in the lower part of the body. The mother is awake to enjoy her baby's birth. But a spinal is usually used for pain relief only during delivery. In a small number of cases it causes severe headaches in the mother during the week after birth or a sharp drop in blood pressure during delivery.

Both epidural and caudal methods cut down on these difficulties. They are not injected directly into the spinal column but into the canal that surrounds it, through a tiny tube threaded through the needle and left in place. Epidural and caudal anesthetic can be used for pain relief during labor as well as during delivery. There is little chance of infection or damage to the spinal cord. These anesthetics are helpful to women with heart conditions, simplifying labor and reducing excess stress and anxiety. However, they can prevent the mother from pushing well and increase the chances of a forceps delivery.

Occasionally a doctor will use other types of regional anesthesia, such as a paracervical or pudendal block. The paracervical is a local anesthetic injected into the nerves of the cervix to eliminate pain from dilation. The woman can still push but may need an additional form of pain relief during delivery. Paracervicals are difficult to administer and only 80 percent successful. The pudendal block deadens the entire vaginal area during delivery, relieving discomfort from the baby's head pushing through.

There's still no perfect form of pain relief that doesn't affect either mother or child. A few obstetricians have been experimenting with acupuncture or hypnosis, and labors have been shortened and eased by vibrators that relax the cervix. If these alternatives to medication become widely available, they may offer the best hope for the future.

In the meantime, the techniques we have on hand have vastly improved obstetric pain relief. "It's true that everything given the mother can affect the baby," says Dr. Fritz Fuchs, chairman of the department of obstetrics and gynecology at the New York Hospital–Cornell

Medical Center. "But it's not true that everything creates a danger, because the way in which we use medications is judicious, and the amount that gets to the fetus is so small that it doesn't present a risk to the fetus. That's what our medical training is all about—using the right thing at the right time in the right place and in the right amount to be helpful and not harmful."

For the most serious childbirth problems, delivery by Caesarean section, too, has made gains over the past. A generation ago, the procedure was considered somewhat dangerous to mother and child. Obstetricians routinely avoided it unless the baby couldn't be delivered any other way. Today the risk from Caesarean section has gone way down. "We don't let patients labor too long because it's so dangerous," says Dr. Rothe. "Generally we'll perform a Caesarean—it involves such a low risk."

Doctors used to make the incision vertically through the abdomen and upper uterine wall. This left a visible scar and the chance that the uterus might rupture before delivery in subsequent pregnancies. Now many physicians make the incision horizontally through the lower part of the uterus in the abdominal crease. This area stretches more easily and is less likely to rupture during another pregnancy. Some doctors will let women with this kind of Caesarean try a natural delivery with their next child. And the scar won't show even under a tiny bikini. Recovery from a Caesarean—which is still considered major surgery—takes longer than for a vaginal delivery, but mothers are now encouraged to be up and around as soon as possible and they stay in the hospital only about a week.

Reducing the Risk to the Newborn

There have been vast improvements in the methods of caring for babies that run into trouble after they are born, as well. In major hospitals and medical centers are intensive-care units for very sick newborns that go far beyond the regular premature nurseries. These facilities have intricate equipment to administer intravenous fluids, test and regulate oxygen intake, monitor heartbeat, breathing, and blood pressure, control respiration, and even adjust the heat of the incubator to the baby's skin temperature. They are staffed by a team that includes nurses and physicians specializing in various aspects of neonatology. Newborn-intensive-care units have made infant death rates fall dramatically, as much as 25 to 50 percent.

More new discoveries to help seriously ill babies are made every day. Newborn-intensive-care units will soon have devices to detect a baby's breathing problems and to stimulate respiration. A machine invented by a West German medical team will let doctors electronically monitor the oxygen levels in a baby's blood continuously without piercing the skin. And doctors are now experimenting with a synthetic hormone which helps prevent respiratory distress in babies before they are born.

Centers for newborn intensive care are being developed to serve entire geographical regions. Women who deliver in less elaborate facilities will have access to the most up-to-date lifesaving devices for their babies. New York Hospital–Cornell Medical Center has an intensive-care unit for high-risk infants that serves nineteen hospitals in the surrounding area. Both New York Hospital and Bellevue–New York University Medical Center have special ambulances with life-support equipment and teams of neonatal nurses, technicians, and physicians. They can move babies from community hospitals to intensive-care facilities while treating them on the way.

The Emotional Side of Childbirth

All of these advances in childbirth seem dazzling, but a bit mechanical and depersonalized. This is a time when tastes and values clamor for making childbearing a warm and natural experience. Some couples will be repulsed by the vision of being surrounded by numerous machines and dials. Adding to the sense of malaise is the whole slant of obstetrics. Obstetricians treat normal pregnancies, of course, but their expertise is geared toward dealing with the things that go wrong, seeing the side of having a baby that is the pathological instead of the normal. And hospitals are primarily places for people who are very sick. While older parents in particular might need this kind of care, it can encourage negative thinking.

Fortunately, the obstetrical field has begun to dispel some of the unpleasant side effects of advanced childbearing technology. The hospital-based midwife programs are a step in this direction. Several hospitals have set up special childbearing centers where labor and delivery take place in friendly and homelike surroundings.

Flower and Fifth Avenue Hospital in New York City gives this description of its Family Living Room:

A combination labor-delivery room incorporating homelike surroundings and all necessary equipment. This room is used for both labor and delivery, avoiding the unnecessary stress caused by transferring the mother to a delivery room during the final stages of labor. The Family Living Room is furnished with easy chairs, radio, television, books and magazines. It is also equipped with a special labor-delivery bed that can be adjusted to various heights. Delivery will take place in the same bed—with or without stirrups. The expectant father or another person of the mother's choice may stay throughout.

Many other hospitals throughout the country now offer "family-centered" maternity care, which tries to make childbirth in standard maternity facilities more of a close family event. According to a couple's needs and choice, the father is usually allowed into the labor and delivery room to participate in the birth process. Some hospitals remove restrictions on the father's visiting hours and encourage him to join the mother in caring for the baby. Family-centered facilities frequently have arrangements for "rooming in," in which the babies can stay with their mothers instead of in the hospital nursery.

Hospitals with family-centered maternity care are often the same ones that offer classes in prepared childbirth and early parenthood. These, too, help a couple understand what is going on around them and the purpose of all those strange instruments. The couple who know what they want and what to expect can take a much more active part in the childbearing process. They are less likely to feel intimidated by intricate equipment or a nurse's clinical attitude. To the extent that a man and woman are well informed, they can do a great deal to stay on top of the situation.

How you react to childbirth will also depend on your choice of hospitals and doctors. Don't assume, for example, that a hospital with the latest lifesaving equipment has the most cold and sterile atmosphere. Some of the country's leading obstetrical centers were the first among conventional hospitals to offer family-centered care.

Even the image of the cold and condescending obstetrician is becoming outdated. Growing numbers encourage breast feeding and prepared childbirth and anticipate working with educated and intelligent patients. "What is encouraging," wrote Rita Kramer, who researched new obstetrical developments for *The New York Times*, "is that obstetricians are becoming increasingly aware of the woman's emotional needs as well as her physical ones, of the need to balance the new technology with old-fashioned tender loving care. It's not the use of machines that's dehumanizing but the way they are used and for what purpose. Not the machine but the human imagination is the deciding factor." With the right obstetrician and hospital, a couple now can have the best of both worlds, the high technology of the hospital and the warmth and satisfaction of the drug-free home birth.

With all these advances, the dangers of childbearing for older women have been grossly exaggerated. Under proper obstetrical care, even the most complicated pregnancy can be turned into a success. Only in the area of conception have the effects of age proved difficult to control. There, as Dr. Sherwin A. Kaufman points out, "age as it relates to fertility is the one factor over which neither doctor nor patient has any control, nor is there any way to reverse it."

It is hoped that the future will turn up more infertility treatments or a new breed of medical wizards who can undo the years of wear and tear on the body. Even so, there's a lot going today for the couple who wants to wait. We need no longer panic when we turn thirty, thirty-five, or forty. Let's replace all those fears about older parenthood with confidence and a reasonable sense of caution.

4

After the Baby's Born: How Does the Late-Blooming Family Fare?

While the medical questions surrounding pregnancy are the most pressing for older parents, the book is by no means closed when a healthy baby arrives. Giving birth is but a small first step toward the formation of a complete human being. After the birth of our daughter, my husband said, "Labor and delivery were easy. Now comes the hard part—raising her." Surely, the most challenging aspect of parenthood follows the first nine months.

This is true for all parents, young or old. As they watch their children grow, they will face the same set of problems—steering through the "terrible twos," instilling discipline and a sense of values, teaching how to share and accept responsibility, to name a few. These child-rearing problems are universal, but others vary with the parents' socio-economic backgrounds and personalities. What about older parents? How will their age affect the way their children are raised? If being older helps them handle certain problems, does it create others? In raising a child from infancy to adulthood, exactly what should older parents expect?

How Much Energy Does It Take?

Young children require an enormous outlay of time and effort. New parents frequently complain of loss of sleep and long hours absorbed by child care. Daily tasks must be rescheduled around the children's timetable and youngsters have a way of turning the most orderly routine into pure chaos. The constant presence of children leaves little free time or privacy.

Can older parents meet such demands? One of the most common charges against them is that they "lack the energy" to cope with young children. This feeds into the other pressures for starting families young. Dr. Mark Flapan, studying women's childbearing motivations, found the fear of being too old to relate to or care for a child typified by this woman's confession:

> I feel as if somebody is . . . whispering in my ear that you better hurry up because there really isn't much time left and you don't want to be sixty years old when your baby is four. You don't want to be an aged parent. If you do have children, you want to be able to physically and emotionally share in some of the activities of the child and if you're . . . forty years old, you're going to be too tired to do anything.

What exactly do we mean by "energy"? Having a child places demands on parents that are both physical and psychological, and many people loosely use "energy" for the resources it takes to meet both. It is widely believed that an individual's capacity to withstand stress diminishes once he or she passes the physical prime. But we also know that each person has a different level of physical and emotional tolerance. This is bound to have more effect than age on the way one handles child rearing.

Physically, there is enormous variation in our store of stamina. Some of the older parents I met were vigorous and athletic to begin with. The ones who enjoyed physical activity ran around with their children a great deal. Those in the sedentary mold, on the other hand, preferred to communicate with their children in more passive fashion. I found these parents' basic body orientation the major influence on the way they related to child rearing.

Many "runners" and "sitters" believed they had the same amount of stamina as in their twenties. "I'm a person of limited energy in a way," said the senior editor, who had teenage children and was still slim and vivacious in her late forties. "I don't think I would have had more energy when I was younger. Yet I found in the hospital I was one of the most vigorous people there. I really looked younger than I was. One's attitude about being old has much more to do with how you feel than your actual age." A former actress who started her family of four in her thirties was accustomed to a slower pace. "I never had tremendous physical energy and have always been the sedentary type," she said. "That's why I found having children difficult."

I did encounter older parents who felt their ability to withstand fatigue had declined since their twenties. But they were unsure if this made any difference in the way they dealt with their children. "You do have less physical energy than a twenty-year-old," said a specialist in international affairs and a first-time mother at thirty-five. "But you may have more emotional staying power to compensate. I tell friends of mine who are older and want children that children really demand a great deal of physical energy and you have to call on other things to make up the difference."

An elementary-school teacher who had her son at thirty-seven was firmly convinced she would have found infant care easier if she were ten years younger. "I found it so hard—I just didn't have the energy to cook, clean, and shop after getting home from work. My husband helped, but there was still so much to do." But I've heard the same story from many young parents. Scheduling all the household tasks, infant care, and a full-time job into one day is hard enough at any age—and may be too much for many twenty-five-year-olds.

How much physical stamina is "enough" to care for young children? And if it does slip away with the years, at what point does this make a difference? One physician, who gave birth to two sons in her thirties, believed anyone in good health had enough stamina to cope with young children, regardless of age. "Some older women might complain of low energy, but I haven't found this true of anyone who is healthy," she said. "If you think that children are causing fatigue, you should check yourself out medically."

Suppose, for whatever reason, you don't have what it takes to run around all day with a child. Or you prefer your easy chair to playing catch in the great American tradition. Does this mean you won't be able to be a good parent? Not necessarily, believes psychiatric social worker and former family counselor at Maimonides Hospital in New York, Sharon Yellin Glick. "The parent up to a certain age essentially determines the children's lifestyle," she says. "Children are basically flexible people who will feel comfortable if Daddy doesn't play ball as long as he explains to them the reason why. I think children don't necessarily need and can even resent this business of playing a lot with them. Some parents identify too much with their children through activities such as Little League. They may be doing that for their own needs, to compensate for what they missed as children."

What about the psychological repercussions of parenthood? How well can older couples handle "emotional fatigue"? Won't they be easily unnerved by screaming or crying? Might they lack the flexibility to cope with youngsters' shifting needs? Here, too, age alone doesn't make a firm dividing line and a great deal hinges on the parents' personalities.

What pop medicine calls Type A's (nervous, aggressive, hard-driving personalities) will have a lower level of tolerance than Type B's (those with placid, low-key dispositions). The older parents I interviewed who were relatively easygoing were less easily upset by children than the ones who were high-strung. One admittedly compulsive woman, now in university administration, explained her reaction to her infant daughter. "I don't think being older affected the way I adjusted," she said. "It would have been difficult for me in any case, because I'm nervous and compulsive. If things fall short of perfection, I fall apart."

The greatest challenge to older parents may come in the initial adjustment to the presence of the child. A couple who delays having children has had many years to develop ingrained habits that are difficult to break. They've grown accustomed to doing what they want when they want.

"When you wait you're so set in the way you do things," said a historian who had her first child six years after her wedding. "You're used to having as much time as you want to put into your job or housework. Once you have a baby, you have to fit everything into a few hours. That's hard after all those years of freedom. If you were younger when you had children, it might be easier to plunge right into it and you'd be less likely to miss all the time that children take up."

Her view was shared by Dr. Edward Waters, who studied 649 New Jersey women who had their first child after the age of thirty-five. In his article "Pregnancy and Labor Experience of Elderly Primigravida" in the *American Journal of Obstetrics and Gynecology*, he said:

> The older patient, in the absence of complications, has neither more nor greater ills in early pregnancy . . . The most disturbing states tend to develop after discharge to her home. If she has married late, the dislocation is less. If childbearing came late in her married life, then the interference with long established routine is notable, and markedly augmented should infant care become complicated.

While older couples may have a somewhat harder transition to parenthood, they can draw on resources that may make coping with children easier in the long run. One way they compensate is by summoning their patience and maturity, bolstered by the realization that their child was wanted and planned for. According to Virginia Barber and Merrill Maguire Skaggs, who studied women's reactions to motherhood, "We learned that women who became mothers in their late twenties and thirties, rather than younger, often found the frustrations of living with an infant more tolerable, perhaps because the child was more intensely desired, or because they had a more mature view of time or of their life and goals."

The type of family style common to older parents also makes living with children easier. Fewer older mothers become full-time housewives than women who have children in their teens and twenties. The older women are more likely to continue working or to keep up interests that take them outside the home. Such activities act as pressure valves that can make the time spent with children seem more enjoyable.

Also, an older couple usually have the financial means to ease child-rearing burdens. They are likely to have funds for household help or for sitters on workdays and evenings out. "Money can make a big difference," said a biologist who became a father at thirty-five. "I think of my younger colleagues with children. The wife has dropped out of work and they're all trying to meet the mortgage, car payments, and milk bills on one salary. Every time they want to go out they have to make an elaborate calculation: 'Well, we'll have to spend $6 for movie tickets and another $6 for a sitter. Throw in two drinks—$5—that's $17! We'd better stay home and watch TV.' These people never get out. They're in the house with the kids morning, noon, and night."

Older parents generally have small families—one child or two—and family size can make a big difference in parental performance. Many parents believe that the tensions created by children grow larger with each addition. "It's not just a matter of doing two loads of diapers at the same time," a social worker and older mother of two explained. An attorney in his mid-forties with two preschoolers had worked out a formula: "Everything goes up in geometric progression, so two children are four times as hard as one." His contention is open to debate, but whether two children are one and a half, two, or four times the work of one, older parents usually keep their family size within a manageable range.

Whatever the number of children desired, the load can ease somewhat with careful planning. Many parents prefer an interval of two and a half years between each child. By that time the oldest is usually toilet-trained and amenable to reasoning. Developmentally, he or she has grown more independent of the parents and can enjoy the company of peers. (From the standpoint of birth defects and complications of pregnancy, it's safer medically, too.) But suppose an older couple wants several children and they don't have enough time to wait for the oldest to reach this stage? Again, how a couple reacts to each new child is a very individual matter.

Spokesmen for spacing children close together point

out that it gets the most difficult phase of child rearing "over with" quickly. There are couples who don't mind two toddlers in diapers at the same time and who prefer children near enough in age to be close companions. "There probably is no one 'best' spacing for all families," says Dr. T. Berry Brazelton, professor of pediatrics at Harvard Medical School. "I would urge parents to plan the second child with an eye to their own tolerance and energy." Those interested in more than one child might want to think about which spacing strategy will work best for them.

An Only Child?

Often an only child and older parents go hand in hand. It may be that, by delaying pregnancy, a couple has run out of time to fit more than one child in. Or that the type of people who wait to have children are primarily interested in the experience of having a child rather than in building a large family. If they're high-powered career types, one child may be all their jobs can accommodate. Many of the older parents I met had only one child, and this practice is on the upswing throughout the country.

Until recently, society frowned on one-child families. Only children have been stigmatized as being spoiled, lonely, and maladjusted, unable to share with other children or accept life's ups and downs. G. Stanley Hall, a prominent American psychologist around the turn of the century, said, "Being an only child is a disease in itself." The cure for the "disease" was to have another child.

Such beliefs led many parents to have additional children for the sake of family balance rather than desire for the children themselves. The family that didn't conform was eyed suspiciously. When the parents of the only child were older to boot, it cast delaying parenthood in an even more unfavorable light.

"I think that one of the reasons we enjoy our daughter so much is because we have only one child," said a college instructor and activist in the women's movement. A statement like that used to be branded pure blasphemy. But recent research has challenged the traditional only-child stereotype, and even suggests an only child enjoys distinct advantages.

It's now believed that an only child tends to be more secure than other children because he or she doesn't have to compete with brothers and sisters for the parents' affection. According to Dr. Murray Kappelman, professor of pediatrics at the University of Maryland Medical School, "The only child has a youth period which is free of the often perplexing problem of sibling rivalry. As the second child arrives on the scene, there is a natural tendency for the two to begin vying for the parents' attention and affection . . . the resentment of the younger sibling for drawing away the parents' attentiveness at times can become overwhelming and can create a very real block to a healthy future sibling relationship. The only child has none of this—there is no competition for a parent's time, no rivalry for affection."

Dr. Kappelman adds, "Additionally, the only child can be himself at all times because of the lack of this internal vying of sibling rivalry. The only child is his own marker. His level of accomplishments is judged by standards not dictated by other siblings but created by the potential and effort of the child."

Studies have shown that only children are less dependent when away from home and get along better with their peers than do children from larger families. Only children are also less likely to suffer emotional problems and more likely to be high achievers. A disproportionate number of only children and firstborns have high IQ's and are on the list of *Who's Who in America*.

"I found that only children are a unique combination of traits typical of firstborn children, such as high intelligence and achievement motivation, as well as some good traits of last borns, such as independence and trustworthiness," says Dr. Toni Falbo, assistant professor of psychology at Wake Forest University, who studied three hundred only children between the ages of seventeen and sixty-two. "One reason that only children are more independent, more trustworthy, and have better verbal IQ's may be that they spend more time with their parents during their formative years, and thus learn more adult-like behavior," she believes.

Whether or not the only child will make the most of such advantages depends a great deal on the attitude of the parents. According to Dr. Michael Lewis, director of the Infant Laboratory of the Educational Testing Service in Princeton, "You can't really ask whether it's good or bad to be an only child. It depends on what your goals are for the child. The special qualities of the only child may not be due to the fact that he's an only child but to the nature of the parents themselves. They may be more egocentric, less family oriented, not willing to give up pleasures of their own for the sake of raising children, and they may impart their own values to their only child, who becomes the typical spoiled brat. I'd speculate that when this personality type develops it's not the absence of other children in the family but the nature of the parents themselves that is the determining factor."

Dr. Kappelman recommends that parents of an only child first of all restrain themselves from overindulgence. "Like any other child, the only child must be made aware that his parents are special in their own right, with lives of their own . . . and activities that are not always shared—in essence, individuals who are both independent and interdependent. If the only child is to feel comfortable about the ultimate need to separate from his parents in order to develop his own personality, the sense of parental independence and individuality is essential."

He and other authorities also suggest that parents of only children make special efforts to expose their children to the company of peers. By encouraging their child to play with others in the neighborhood or by sending the child at an early age to play groups and nursery school, they can teach the child how to get along with others. "If there is a disadvantage to being an only child, it's being isolated," said Margaret Mead, whose only child, a daughter, was born when she was thirty-eight. "You have to find ways to get the only child together with other children of different ages—cousins, neighbors . . . My daughter is an only child and she has an only child. I always saw to it that she was involved in enough hassles with other children."

How did the older parents I interviewed feel about having only one child? On the whole, they were enthusiastic, but did see some weak spots. Several regretted that their children had to seek playmates from outside the home but differed on whether onliness was an obstacle to making friends. One specialist in international affairs, whose son was born when she was thirty-five, felt he could relate well to both adults and peers. "At school they said Seth was a very adult child—but he was still a child," she said. "He manages with both adults and peers. He has rather successful social relationships."

"An only child and child of older parents has much more pressure put on him to make it socially—all the effort has to be on their part," she believes. "They may actually develop social skills other children don't have to. But there is the loneliness and the worrying that if anything happens he has to cope alone. He needs assurance he has a place to go."

A high-school teacher who fathered a son in his late thirties told me, "I really don't sit around and think, 'He's an only child.' I don't see him with the tag 'only child.' If I see him becoming self-centered, I discipline him. I think you'll find that we discipline Matthew much more for self-centeredness than a family that has three kids."

He felt that raising an only child was easier in certain localities. "In the city we had to make appointments for every kid he played with," he said. "Here in the suburbs there are all sorts of children out in the street. It may even be easier to have an only child in the suburbs and more than one in the city. In the suburbs you'd be spending all your time chauffeuring four kids to various activities and dentist appointments. In the city when they become eight or ten they can take the bus or subway themselves."

No family size can be entirely trouble free, and each combination of parents and children has its own set of problems. In any event, the one-child family is coming into its own as an attractive and acceptable family form. The thought of being able to fit only one child in should not deter a couple from having a child later in life.

"The problem is the idea people have that they should either have no children or have two as a minimum," says Dr. E. James Lieberman, chief of the Center for Studies of Child and Family Mental Health at the National Institute of Mental Health. "Nobody should feel they have to have two . . . We have to make delayed parenthood and the one-child family respectable. As a matter of fact, parents who are older, better educated, and established in life are more likely to be busy, active, creative people, less likely to have a need to live their lives through their children, which is probably better for the children in the long run. I'm not saying that everyone should necessarily stop at one, just that we should add the one-child family to the range of possible alternatives."

Parents and Peers

As a child grows older, his or her contacts with other children become increasingly important. Does having older parents affect a child's relationship with peers?

When I spoke with older parents and children of older couples, I had the distinct impression the parents were more sensitive about their age than their children were.

No one was ashamed of the fact that he or she was older than the parents of the children's friends. But several did wonder if their children made such comparisons. "Richard knows our age," one writer said. "For years I wouldn't tell him—I didn't want him to go out on the street and tell everyone my age. So I used to say I was 150, knowing full well he wouldn't believe me and he would think the whole thing was ridiculous."

Several parents recounted incidents where someone mistook their status. The university administrator, who was a first-time mother at thirty-nine, recalled, "Henry and I took our daughter to a football game when she was about a year old. As I was putting some extra wraps on her, a woman behind me tapped me on the shoulder and said, 'What a devoted grandmother you are!' " The same thing happened to some of the fathers as well.

Variations of the grandparent theme easily crop up—and the message doesn't have to be explicit. One couple needed no reminding. They were both college professors in their late thirties with a four-year-old son. "All our colleagues started having children during their twenties," they said. "Now their kids are in high school or college. So around them sometimes we *feel* like grandparents."

Did these older parents feel they stood out like sore thumbs in the company of parents fifteen years their junior? Not exactly, but many did sense some discomfort in dealings with parents of their children's friends. "Most of the women I met in the park were ten years younger," said the social worker, who had her children in her late thirties. "When I finally met a mother in her thirties, we embraced."

What was it about younger mothers that was so irritating? A specialist on early childhood education and first-time mother at thirty-seven tried to put her finger on it. "Friendships just didn't grow," she said. "It wasn't a question of mothers who worked versus those who didn't—the others were just a lot younger. There is a kind of communication that has to do with age and greater comfort from people your own age. I found an unseasoned quality among women in their twenties, a kind of arrogance."

Several women felt that age differences were less significant than how other women handled their motherhood role. A former actress and literature teacher who worked ten years before starting a family tried to keep abreast of developments in the arts and current affairs while her children were young. The younger mothers she met had no interests besides their children. "I had a terrible time adjusting," she said. "I was just bored with diaper talk. I could stand it only for about the first few weeks of chit and chat. I felt terribly maladjusted and thought something was wrong with me. When we entertained, the women sat on one side of the room and made diaper talk. The men sat on the other side and talked about the things I was interested in."

Another woman with a Ph.D. in political science reported success in finding mothers in their twenties with concerns like hers. "It depends on what kind of lifestyle they lead," she said. "If they're professional women, it's easy for me to get along with them. You tend to choose some of your friends because their child can play with your child. But particularly as Peter grows older, we are seeking out people who have more in common with us than just the fact that they have children."

She also believed having a young child helped narrow the age gap with the parents of her son's friends. "People think I'm younger because I have a young child. I'm entering middle age and have a young feeling because we have to cope with a young child, and my husband feels the same way. You're treated as if you're a lot younger, and your friends are younger."

Most of the other parents I interviewed chose their friends on the basis of similar interests and lifestyle. Many did make it a point to single out other older couples with children. The ones who usually had the hardest time with peers were the women who spent much of their time at home. They had more opportunity to run into the types who entered parenthood much younger in more restricted parental roles.

I don't think that peer relations among parents themselves is one of the burning issues of child rearing or delayed parenthood. But if you prefer to associate with other like-minded people and feel this is important to you, where you live can make a difference. Said two attorneys who had their first child when the husband was in his early forties, "We went to our first PTA meeting at Simon's nursery school. We thought we were unique, but almost everyone there was just like us. People in New York get married so much later and have kids so much later—and there are so many only children." Had they attended that PTA meeting in the suburbs or out in the country, the reverse might have been true. There, for the most part, the traditional family styles are still going strong.

How did the children feel about their parents' age? Most were unaware of it. The few who were aware seemed to feel it made little difference. One thirteen-year-old son of a physician in his late fifties said, "Dad is a lot older." I asked him if he was older because of the way he looked, thought, or acted. "The way he looks, but not the way he acts or thinks," the boy said. "I wish he were younger," he added but couldn't think of what would be different if he were. A young woman born when her mother was forty-four recalled she was oblivious to her parents being older. "What bothered me," she said, "was not my friends noticing my parents were different but my relationships with my cousins—they were all old enough to be aunts and uncles. I didn't know what to call them."

According to Dr. Lee Salk, "Most children could not care less about how old their parents are. But if you feel ashamed of being past forty, or feel old, this will reflect itself in your children's attitude. They will sense your embarrassment and your attempt to fight advancing years or to deny you're getting older by having children . . . Other children might tease yours about having older parents, but such taunts are relatively unimportant to them, especially if your relationship is solid and loving."

Are Children of Older Parents Different?

Do the children of older parents stand out? Are they somehow different? Unfortunately, the subject hasn't been well studied. I asked child psychiatrist Dr. Shirley Van Ferney if she has found a disproportionate number of children of older parents among her patients. "No," she said. "I haven't found the parents' age makes any difference in these problems, and I really haven't noticed any different problems among children of older parents."

Some specialists believe that older parents' relationship with their children tends to be more intense. According to Dr. Virginia Lozzi, associate in psychiatry at the Columbia Presbyterian Medical Center, "Older parents, especially with their firstborn, may tend to over-emphasize all aspects of their relationship. Since it is not too likely that the thirty-five-year-old mother will have a second baby, parents may lavish too much love and attention on their child. They may become overpermissive, overprotective, or overcritical of their offspring. This 'overlove' may suffocate the child."

The only child of older parents is especially vulnerable to overprotectiveness. If parents are too old to have another child or have settled on having only one, there can be a kind of "putting all one's eggs into one basket" effect. "I think this is true of the mother who has had a difficult time getting pregnant or has had trouble with miscarriages," says Dr. Van Ferney. "There's a phrase for it—anticipatory grief—you're so afraid of losing the child."

When this happens, says Dr. Lee Salk, "the child can become anxious and tense. Or if he or she is constantly told not just to be careful, which makes sense, but 'Be careful when you climb, you'll fall' or 'When you get into the elevator, make sure the doors don't close on your bicycle'—contingencies that don't naturally occur to a child—you are in danger of making him overly vigilant and too frightened to move away from you. The child is then handicapped emotionally because he is unwilling to experience change, reluctant to try new things. He will tend to stick to what is familiar and safe, becoming fixated at a certain stage of growth and not able to go on to the next."

This is something, however, which parents can watch out for and keep under control. "I think we can recognize when the very natural protective instinct begins to interfere with a child's capacity to explore freely or try new experiences," Dr. Salk adds. And the danger of overprotectiveness is hardly limited to older parents.

One couple, very active in political life, had the chance to compare late and early parenthood on a personal level. They had two children in their early forties, a "second family" after their first set of children had left home. "These children are growing up much more quickly," the father said. "They could do more at an earlier age—walk, talk—and are brighter. I think it's because they're around adults all the time. All our friends have children who are grown up."

We don't yet have enough information to tell if his observation applies to all families of older parents. So many factors go into building a child's intellectual potential that it's hard to single out parental age. Research has shown that outstanding achievers with high IQ's are most often firstborns, only children, and children from small families, and they are more common to late-blooming parents. But the studies to date of the relationship between parents' age and the child's intellectual performance are still inconclusive.

Illness and Death

Insurance companies thrive on these facts: a man aged thirty-five has a one in 9 chance of dying before paying off a twenty-year mortgage. Likewise, a man who has his first child at thirty-five has the same chance of dying before that child reaches full adulthood (the odds are somewhat less for women). Statistically we know that middle age ushers in a higher incidence of fatal or serious illness. So the children of older parents have a somewhat greater chance of losing one or both of them before they are grown.

The death of a parent can be traumatic to a young child, shaking the foundations of family life. Writes Constance M. Dennehy in the *British Journal of Psychiatry*, "The fact of bereavement would mean not only that a child lost a loved person on whom he was dependent and towards whom he might experience conflicting emotions, but also, in so many cases, the total disintegration of the child's environment as he had come to expect and understand it. For so many children the loss of a father results in loss of the mother as an effective parental figure." Numerous studies have shown that there is a higher incidence of depression and other forms of mental illness among people who lost either parent before they were fifteen.

The family will also experience serious shock if either

parent becomes seriously ill. When this happens, pronounced changes occur in the home routine and in the way family members relate to each other and the outside world. According to Dr. E. James Anthony, director of the Eliot Division of Child Psychiatry and Ittleson Professor of Child Psychology at Washington University in St. Louis, "The present-day family, by reason of its small size, its comparative isolation, and its limited services to its members, has been shown to be extremely vulnerable to the strains of illness . . . Serious illness, either mental or physical, is something new and tough that confronts the family and it can certainly be described as traumatic, pressuring and penalizing."

These are bleak facts, but they should be recognized and confronted. How should couples who delay childbearing until they are close to middle age come to terms with the possibility of illness or death? One woman who had a son when she was thirty-five expressed concern about her son's fear of being left alone. "Evan knows we're older than his friends' parents," she said, "and worries something will happen to us and therefore to him." Is this predicament peculiar to older parents and their children?

According to the psychological experts I interviewed, no. "Fear of loss and abandonment is a very real fear to children regardless of the parents' age," says Sharon Yellin Glick. "If the parents have such fears, they're obviously more likely to convey these worries to their children. But these questions pop up with any parent and child. I don't think they're peculiar to older parents. It's more a matter of how each parent deals with his or her stage of development and life issues and how they grow older."

Dr. Van Ferney agrees: "Every child is afraid that his or her parents are going to die. But a parent dying— that can happen at any time, or even when he or she is young."

Most psychological authorities believe that families that are well adjusted from the start are best equipped to confront these crises. This is the key factor, not the parents' chronological age. If parents feel comfortable about their age and accept the eventuality of illness and death without making them into an obsession, they should be able to convey a healthy outlook on the problem to their children. This applies to parents of all ages, not just the latecomers.

The Generation Gap: How Wide?

What happens when the children of older parents grow up and begin to carve out their own lives? This was one of the questions I encountered most often among people curious about delayed parenthood. A typical reaction came from a saleswoman who had her first child at nineteen. "Just imagine the generation gap," she said. "I'm a young mother and there's still a gap between me and my daughter. With older parents there must be a double generation gap!"

Does the generation gap grow wider with the parents' age? Again, like the question of energy, it depends on what you mean by the term. "Generation gap" is commonly used to describe the lack of communication engendered by some form of rebellion of young people in their teens and early twenties against their parents and elders. The term came into its own during the turbulent sixties when rebellious youth created an entire counter-culture to challenge their elders' values and lifestyles. The implication was that our society was changing so rapidly that each generation would have little in common with the one before it.

But with the seventies, the momentum behind the generation gap slowed down. Conditions that brought the tension between the Establishment and its critics to its height have subsided and the sexual revolution has lost its initial sensationalism. Many symbols of the counter-culture have been coopted by its adversaries. Differences in thought, behavior, and values still separate one generation from another. But they don't amount to opposing world views and can't easily be measured by their difference in chronological years.

"I think the generation gap is a bunch of nonsense, a press hype," says Sharon Yellin Glick. She and other psychological authorities believe all young people must pass through a rebellious phase. "I think all kids go through a period of separating and individuating, usually around adolescence," she says. "By separating, they figure out who they are and how to handle their lives." No matter what the parents' age, they can expect some form of rebellion. Says Dr. Van Ferney, "I can work with disturbed kids and get along fine with them. But I predict there will come a time when I won't be able to get along as well with my own kids—they have to rebel against their own parents some time."

Does the magnitude of the rebellion increase with the parents' age? Will the reaction against older parents be more intense? Not necessarily. "The quality of this process will depend on how the child is being raised," says Ms. Glick. "Perhaps culturally the older parent is less in touch with what is in vogue. But if the parent is stable, with a clear sense of self and comfort with his or her lifestyle, he or she could give the child a more sure sense of self. In general, I would think that older parents might have less of a generation-gap problem if they're basically secure and social people." "Sometimes an older parent is more capable of bridging the generation gap," believes Dr. Van Ferney. "If parents are comfortable with their age, the kids will be comfortable, no matter how old the parents are."

Most of the older parents I met felt the same way. "I don't think the generation gap is real. The only generation-gap problem that counts is that older people in many cases are more experienced, more settled, and have a broader view," one first-time father at thirty-six said. "Maybe there is even less of a generation gap with older parents because they have gained the wisdom that they can't teach their child about everything. Had my father practiced what he preached, there wouldn't have been a generation gap in my own home when I was growing up."

Besides bringing accumulated wisdom and a sense of perspective to the generation gap, the age of older parents may force them to develop superior mechanisms to attack the problem. Young parents sometimes try to relate to their teenagers by pretending they're the same age. This blurs the real issue of separation and can confuse the child. The psychological authorities I interviewed felt this was unhealthy. "With a parent who's very young," says Ms. Glick, "there could be too much of a peer struggle."

Older parents can't easily make a pretense of being young. Their age forces them to confront the fact that they are clearly in a different generation. So to relate to their children, they must communicate in other ways. According to Ms. Glick, "If a parent can realize analogous situations from his or her own life and can identify with the problems a child is facing, the parent may be able to minimize the tension. The people who have the worst generation-gap problems are usually the ones who create many barriers to communicating with their children—either the children revolt or they conform entirely."

Instead of a generation gap, experts such as Ms. Glick and Dr. Lee Salk would prefer to talk about a "communication gap." "Parents must acknowledge that their attitude and the way they cope with their own disapproval of the situation are potential problems," said Dr. Salk. "That doesn't mean abandoning what they think is right or moral, but that they see the world through the child's eyes and learn to comprehend—if not embrace—the quickly changing values of modern society . . . The one word of warning I give . . . is never to say to children, 'When I was your age, I never did that.' You should understand your children well enough to know that immediately turns them off. But if you have always shown understanding of them, you will find that they are more than willing and capable of understanding you. And that's the greatest way to overcome many problems."

Older Parents, Older Grandparents

What about the parents of older parents? How will their children's decision to delay parenthood affect them? Suppose a couple doesn't have a child until their mid-thirties. The baby's grandparents will therefore most likely be in their sixties and may have passed from the scene. If so, what difference does this make?

While grandparents are not nearly as critical as parents in a child's development, they still perform important functions. According to Sharon Yellin Glick, "There's a type of alliance between grandparents and grandchildren that has a very special role for a child. The grandparent, as that person goes through the aging process and begins to think about his or her own death, sees himself or herself continuing through the grandchild. Children get much more loving and a fuller sense of the continuity of life from being with the older generation. Grandparents have a giving, loving quality and a sense of approval that parents can't give because they're the ones responsible for disciplining the child."

So grandparents provide a child with another source of love and security, softening the intensity of the parental relationship. And they are one of the child's early educators, imparting knowledge accumulated over many years and a sense of the passage of time. As Margaret Mead once put it, "One of the great appeals of the grand-child-grandparent generation is, as someone has said, 'they have a common enemy.' The older generation's talk about one's own parents when they were children tends to reduce the tendency of adults to announce, 'My father would never have permitted me to.' "

In our highly mobile society, it has become more difficult for grandparents to play these roles. The older and younger generations of one family no longer tend to live under the same roof, as was the rule fifty years ago. Often children today see their grandparents only on ceremonial occasions, such as Christmas, birthdays, and Easter. And the loss of a grandparent is nowhere as devastating as the loss of a parent. Nevertheless, states Dr. Marvin Hader in *Family Process*, "the absence of grand-parental influence can be deleterious to grandchild development." A childhood without grandparents will be more common among the offspring of older parents.

Even if an older couple's parents are alive while their grandchildren are young, their age may affect the type of grandparental role they can play. Gerontologists Bernice L. Neugarten and Karol K. Weinstein found several styles of grandparenting. Grandparents could act like surrogate parents, caring for their grandchildren while their parents worked, or could serve as energetic play-mates or "fun-seekers." They could also present them-selves in more formal, remote roles as older figures of authority and wisdom.

Neugarten and Weinstein observed that during the trend toward younger marriages, there emerged increas-ing numbers of grandparents in their forties and fifties who could act almost as youthful as parents. These types were more likely to assume playful roles. It is likely that few grandparents in the families of older parents, by vir-tue of their advanced age, will be able to grandparent as "fun-seekers." They'll probably appear more often in the more formal grandparental garb.

Eventually older parents will have their turn as grandparents, too. Compared to their own parents, they are more apt to be in their sixties and seventies before their children start families. They, too, will in most cases be too old to qualify as grandparents in the youthful mold and will have an even greater chance of missing out entirely on grandparenthood.

What happens when a couple grows old and the grandchildren don't arrive? Grandparenthood is one of the few things aging adults look forward to. It is considered a just reward for all the hard years of raising one's own brood and the best sweetener for old age. "What right, one may ask, do these aging Americans have to expect grandchildren?" wondered Russell Baker of *The New York Times*. "The answer is that American society has conditioned them to construct their lives on the assumption that grandparenthood is inevitable, and as a class they have done so."

Baker humorously speculated about the effects of what he called "the grandparent shortage, grandchild frustration anxiety."

As the years keep rolling past, the hair keeps getting sparser, the vision keeps getting dimmer and the grandchildren still fail to arrive. All those exercises, that dieting, the skin care, the cosmetics and hair revivers, the soaps faithfully bought because they kept the hands younger—the purpose of all these was to prepare for a glamorous grandparenthood. Eventually, it was understood, people would gaze at the results in amazement and say, "But you're too young to be a grandmother!"

These people were all fitted out for grandparenthood and had nothing to do. They were in a holding pattern between youth and decrepitude. The airport was closed, as it were, to Grandparentville, and it was beginning to look as if they would have to keep circling overhead until the gas ran low and they were rerouted to Octogeneria.

What Baker said was largely in jest but rightly pointed to the frustrations of growing old without grandchildren. Developmentally, grandparenthood is considered a critical experience for the aging adult as well as for the grandchild, a chance to relive the best parts of family life without the responsibility and daily irritations.

A couple who delays parenthood could very well be in for a grandchildless old age. And if they consider grandchildren their due, they may even try to pressure their children into marrying and starting their families while they are young, depriving them of the option to wait as they did. This doesn't have to be inevitable, but it's something an older couple should be aware of.

Late Parents Later in Life

Delaying parenthood generally works to a couple's advantage when their children are young. It gives them time to develop the emotional maturity for parenthood and to amass enough money for housing, medical, and child-care costs. In a few respects, however, an older couple's age may work against them when their children grow up.

One of the main arguments I've heard from couples who want to start their families young is that they'll have many years left to enjoy themselves after their children leave home. By the time an older couple's children have grown up, the parents may not have much time for themselves again. Or their proximity to retirement age may put them under financial strain.

If the parents have had the foresight to plan for their children's education in advance, they should be able to move toward retirement without cramping their style. If they haven't, the costs of college can eat into funds for retirement and other expenses of later years. Late parents may not, for example, be able to help their grown children with major purchases, such as the down payment on a house, a practice that has become increasingly popular. "I'll be at least sixty when my son is about to get married," a freelance researcher and first-time mother at thirty-five predicted. "We won't be able to help him because we'll have to take care of ourselves." In higher income brackets, especially when both parents work, such difficulties will be minimal, but older parents shouldn't neglect to think ahead financially.

If the parents can't take care of themselves, the responsibility for their care may be forced prematurely on their children. Two generations ago, parents often moved in with their children after their children's children had left home. Today, as family ties weaken, the elderly tend to live alone, but their children are usually at a stage in life where they can help with their care. When late parents grow old, their children may be too young to take them in or to subsidize their living expenses.

Some older parents will be facing old age about the time that their children are making the final break from home. Psychologists believe the "empty nest" is a time of trial for many families. Couples who postpone parenthood get to bypass the empty nest during their forties. They'll still be surrounded by young children when other couples are confronting crises such as menopause or the prospect of another twenty-five years alone. This may ease older parents' middle-age growing pains, but they will still encounter the empty nest at a later point in their lives.

The nest of older parents will empty during their late fifties or early sixties, close to the time they will retire. Retirement raises new psychological challenges, for it puts an end to long-standing social ties and the part of one's identity bound up with the job. If the empty nest for older parents coincides with retirement, they could face two life events involving loneliness and loss at the same time.

Observes Robert C. Peck, director of the Research and Development Center for Teacher Education in Austin, Texas:

> The man whose children are grown when he is forty may not yet have experienced the male climacteric; he may be still working "uphill" to master his vocational role; and he may just be entering a widened circle of social, political or other activities, and a widened circle of friends. This makes "the departure of children" a much different thing for this man, than for a man of sixty whose youngest child is just leaving home; who is nearing vocational retirement; whose family and friendship circle has been broken by several deaths; and whose interest or potency in sexual activity may be markedly less than in his earlier years.

How well older parents handle this and other potential problems rests on their individual strengths and weaknesses. In the future, as the proportion of older people in our population rises, the average retirement age may be pushed up to seventy or even seventy-five years. There already is a movement among senior citizens to abolish mandatory retirement at sixty-five. If this takes place, the impact of retirement and the empty nest on older parents will diminish.

Even if current retirement patterns prevail, the family dynamics characteristic of older parents may ease their adjustment to their children's departure. Social scientists researching the American family have found that the most traumatic reactions to the empty nest come from women who are overcommitted to the maternal role. "Women who have overprotective relationships with their children are more likely to suffer depression in their post-parental period than women who do not have such relationships," concluded sociologist Pauline Bart, who studied the sources of depression in women aged forty to fifty-nine. "Housewives have a higher rate of depression than working women . . . Not only do housewives have more opportunity than working women to invest themselves completely in their children, but the housewife is cut down once there are fewer people for whom to shop, cook and clean."

A woman who delays parenthood may be beyond middle age when her children leave home, but she is much less likely than the young housewife-mother to have made them her sole preoccupation. Chances are, she has kept up her job and other extrafamilial activities. And having started childbearing late, she and her husband are apt to have developed a marital relationship that doesn't focus on the children only. Even if their children take off at a sensitive point, older parents should be able to find satisfaction from their investment in each other.

5

Late Parenthood and
the Future

The trend toward older parenthood has just started. How long can we expect it to continue? Since it involves far-reaching changes in family life and the way men and women see themselves, how will it affect our society in the future?

How Much of a Trend?

How much of a trend is prolonging parenthood past the age of thirty? In terms of actual numbers, it's a minority movement and will continue to be so in the years to come. But the minority will grow and we can expect a larger proportion of college-educated couples on the bandwagon. As of 1974, 65,213 women had their first child over thirty, 5 percent of all first-time mothers in this country. Within the next decade I expect the proportion of older mothers to at least double.

As women draw away from an exclusive motherhood role, more will be attracted to having children later, after they've established their identities and careers. For all the reasons that women are joining the work force, families are shrinking, and divorces are growing, the age one begins to have children will continue to rise.

The trend toward late parenthood will also gain momentum from demographic forces. Population experts expect our current low fertility and mortality rates to inflate the proportion of elderly people in our society. If more men and women live longer, this will ease some of the pressure for starting families early. Late parents will have a good chance of living to see their children grown, perhaps as long as young parents do today. Waiting to have children may even become desirable to keep the life cycle in balance.

Futurist Alvin Toffler has speculated that the years to come will find many couples deferring parenthood until they retire. "Once childbearing is broken away from its biological base, nothing more than tradition suggests having children at an early age," he says. But even with scientific advances that could make this possible, delaying parenthood that long is most unlikely. Nor do I expect that large numbers of couples in the foreseeable future will have their first child in their forties.

Most of those who join the ranks of late parents will be in their mid-thirties—thirty-three, thirty-four, thirty-five years old. We'll see larger numbers in their late thirties, too, but the bulk of older parents won't be waiting quite that long. Still, couples delaying childbearing until their thirties are on the upswing, and even those prone to plunge into parenthood earlier will hesitate longer than they have before.

Historically speaking, later marriage and parenthood aren't new. Before the Industrial Revolution, late marriages by current standards were prevalent in Europe—a couple had to prove they had the property and means of livelihood to support themselves before starting out on their own. This was also a form of birth control, since delayed marriages helped limit family size. Today, late marriages are still common in Ireland and are encouraged in countries such as China to stem the birth rate.

There have been precedents for older parenthood in this country, too. For example, the average marriage age for men born in 1866 was 27.32 years and for women 24.08 years. But from about 1890 until the late 1950's the trend was toward marriage and parenthood at an earlier age. The movement in the opposite direction that is going on now appears especially striking against the backdrop of the 1950's, the era of the "feminine mystique" that glorified early marriage, large families, and women in the kitchen.

In a sense, the current trend toward postponing the formation of a family touches on some of the fundamental reasons why couples marry late. Men and women are now re-examining some of the old economic considerations for waiting to start a family. And delaying parenthood usually acts as a brake on family size.

But today's older parents also reflect developments that are entirely new. Most outstanding is the change in women's roles. With new outlets in careers, their horizons no longer end with the household. The primary reason for delaying parenthood today is to give them and their husbands the freedom to fashion their own mix of work and family life.

New, too, are the technological breakthroughs that make late parenthood easier and safer than ever before. Our current contraceptive practices can effectively regulate the timing of children and family size. Advances in genetics and obstetrics have removed most of the hazards of childbirth beyond the optimal reproductive age. The feasible choices of family style open to couples today have never been greater.

Even if older parents remain in the minority, they are in the vanguard of changes that are transforming the

American family in general. The average family is already shrinking in size. Families of older parents will be even smaller and will help popularize the one- or two-child ideal.

With fewer children, men and women will be spending a smaller portion of their lives in child rearing. Women in particular will have more freedom to pursue activities and interests apart from motherhood; they'll develop less family-oriented identities. Social commentators already speak of motherhood as an "occupation facing decline." Many more women like today's older mothers will emerge, and the arguments for combining work and family will grow stronger. Even women who have children in their twenties will come closer to the older-mother profile.

Having a child is considered one of the major life events for a human being, and the age one becomes a parent affects the timing of the developmental phases that follow. When custom called for having children young, social commentators observed the emergence of the four-generation family—parents in their twenties with young children, grandparents in their forties or fifties, great-grandparents in their seventies. One entered each stage of adult life increasingly early, so that the whole maturation process accelerated.

If more couples delay parenthood until their thirties, the four-generation family will disappear. A three-generation pattern will be in vogue again and the pace of adult development will slow down. This will affect how old a person acts and feels. According to Bernice L. Neugarten, Joan W. Moore, and John C. Lowe, who studied the aging process, "There exists what might be called a prescriptive timetable for the ordering of major life events: a time in the life span when men and women are expected to marry, a time to raise children, a time to retire . . . Age norms and age expectations operate as prods and brakes upon behavior, in some instances hastening an event, in others delaying it. Men and women are aware not only of the social clocks that operate in various areas of their lives, but they are aware of their own timing, and readily describe themselves as 'early,' 'late,' or 'on time' with regard to family and occupational events."

We can define our age biologically, but we define it socially as well. And what society deems appropriate behavior for any age will change from time to time. Should delayed parenthood become popular enough, people who have their first child in their thirties won't be considered late at all. Even if they remain in the minority, the trend toward postponing family formation is bound to affect our definitions of old and young.

As this practice becomes acceptable, many of the misconceptions and prejudices about older parents will disappear. The first-time expectant mother with graying hair will no longer feel out of place in her doctor's office, nor will she be mistaken for the grandmother of her child. It's possible that the stigma of ill-timed parenthood will be transferred to the other extreme—toward parents who are too young. Doctors will direct their fire against the teenage mother for the high risks she takes with her child. We'll wonder more about how much maturity it takes to have children than about how much energy; we'll speculate on how the children of teenage parents feel about mothers and fathers who are so young.

The Long Run

Does the trend toward delayed parenthood augur well for the future? Who will reap its benefits? Surely it will help the feminist cause, making it easier for women to combine career and motherhood. Observes Professor Jessie Bernard, "If provision can be made for women to have their children young and then proceed in a normal and acceptable way to professional or other careers, youthful marriages may be a good thing; but if we are going to continue to punish women for the time taken out to have babies, later marriage may be preferable."

So far, most of the women who have delayed parenthood are an elite group. They've had the best educations and access to the most promising jobs our society has to offer. If they work, it's often out of choice. They can afford expensive housekeepers and high-quality child care that is way beyond the reach of the average working woman. We can't expect all women to end up as they have—there just aren't enough high-paying jobs or reliable housekeepers to go around.

If all women are to be truly liberated, we'll have to change the way work and household responsibilities are organized. I recently met a female law-school professor who was asked by a prominent foundation developing policies to improve the status of women, "Is there anything else we can do?" "Change the way *men's* work is defined," she replied. "If the men have jobs that demand so much of their time, how can they help out at home? And if women are competing for the same jobs as men, how will they have enough time to fit their families in?"

Some of the older mothers privileged enough to have the right amount of money and the right kind of job have been able to fit families in. But most American women can't. If they're to attain equality, we'll need jobs for men and women that recognize their needs as parents; we'll need a system of quality child care accessible to all; we'll have to redefine male and female roles. To date, says Mirra Komarovsky, professor emeritus of sociology at Barnard College, "the great number of women in the labor force has not yet produced the necessary social inventions."

It's been argued that if the pressures for social change are intense enough, our institutions will bend to accommodate them. The older mothers who have successfully combined work and family are actually working within the constraints of our social system as it is. Instead of struggling to make our institutions more hospitable to working women, they're able, in a sense, to "buy" their way out. Observed University of California sociologist Arlie Hochschild, who had her first child at thirty-one, "It's a private solution to a public problem. I don't think, 'Lucky me, I've scampered around the system.' My feeling is that we need to change the occupational system itself." What effect will older working mothers have? Will the example they set encourage other women to come to terms with our social system as it is? Or will it spur the drive for sexual equality?

Professor Cynthia Fuchs Epstein believes the outcome will be positive. "The arrangements these older women make that skirt around the fundamental changes that are necessary aren't going to threaten the women's movement," she said. "Being a working mother is still no bed of roses, even for them. Most women who work don't have money and can't get high-quality child care. Changes are going to have to be made because the vast majority of working women still need them. These high-level working mothers are still the most articulate spokesmen for women's rights and they serve as role models for the rest of the women trying to raise families and work. What they do, however they arrange their child care, still helps legitimate the activities of working-class women."

We can expect delayed parenthood to be applauded by advocates of women's rights, but Columbia University sociologist Amitai Etzioni is troubled by other long-term consequences. Examining the social implications of our growing body of genetic knowledge in his book *Genetic Fix*, he observes, "In the rush to promote birth control, we did not emphasize as much as we could have that the best of all possible worlds—both for the family and for society—was to be achieved not only by having fewer children but by having them earlier . . . The un-witting damage caused by the anti-population propa-ganda, which advocates delayed parenthood, was a typi-cal case in point where the concern with one dimension —overpopulation—was not balanced to another, here, genetic health."

Wouldn't amniocentesis and early abortion eliminate the danger of genetic defects in children of older couples? Not altogether, Etzioni believes.

> If all or most of those parents who discover they have a defective fetus will decide to abort it and will try to have another child (while those who would give birth to a defective child would be less likely to try to have more children), there might be a problem. Since many genetic illnesses do not hit each offspring (e.g., sickle cell anemia), the next fetus (or the one after that) may be normal and live to reproductive age—but with the capacity to pass on the latent defective gene to its off-spring. Hence, if most afflicted fetuses, which, without intervention, would not have reached reproductive age —are replaced by fetuses that are "normal" in all but their hidden, inactive, sick gene, the gene pool will only get dirtier . . . If public health authorities would urge parents to complete childbearing when the mother is young and the rate of genetic illness is therefore signif-icantly lower, this could make up for all, or at least part, of the "deterioration" of the pool caused by the genetic interventions which increased the numbers of reces-sive, sick genes.

Professor Etzioni is disturbed by the genetic effect on future generations of prolonging parenthood.

But is having children at the optimal reproductive age altogether in society's best interests? Should we make what is biologically right socially right? I asked Dr. Zonia Krassner, associate professor of biology at the State

University of New York College at Old Westbury and a specialist in developmental genetics. "Biology is not our destiny," she said. "But let's look at our biology: let's not pretend we're not animals. We are primates. Being humans, we're intensely flexible, much more so than other animals. But I do feel certain things overtax our biology too much. There are costs, physical and psychological, when we do this. We don't know enough about the human being as an animal yet to be able to tell the costs of all these alternatives.

"I'm ambivalent about going beyond the biologically optimal age because I see the total picture. Biologically, the optimal time for reproduction is between twenty and thirty. Psychologically, women in our society, for a variety of reasons, aren't ready for parenthood until they are twenty-six or older. People during much of their twenties also aren't ready economically to provide the setting a child needs. Socially, there's an age problem— the marriages aren't sufficiently stable at that point. If these things are so important, you can't live according to a biological optimum.

"What I plead for is that women try not to wait until the last moment, when they're over thirty-five. Amniocentesis, natural childbirth, proper obstetrical care can minimize the hazards to the child of older parents, but basically, you have a trade-off. From a long-term perspective, we face background radiation and an ever-increasing onslaught of additives and other substances from our polluted atmosphere. We don't yet know how mutagenic they are. This is something I'm vaguely concerned about but it's not my primary focus. I'm concerned that we shouldn't burden future generations, but we shouldn't be in debt to them either.

"I do feel we should pay more attention to our biological background. For example, I'm a great proponent of nursing. There's every indication that it's infinitely superior to cow's milk. If that is so important, why can't we arrange our society so fathers can participate in diapering and care for the baby while the women are allowed to nurse for a year. Let's not put such demands on women that they feel they are failing their professions and themselves. If we are stuck with something we can change, let's change it.

"There's a price to pay for being a woman in our society and in many others as well. Whatever the decision you make, if you have children late there's a price to pay in health risks. If you have them too young, there's a price to pay in not knowing yourself. But we can try to make the price of our own choosing. And knowing the risks, we can work for a society that will minimize these risks."

It may be that we'll eventually have a society that will let women have children at whatever age they wish without penalty to their personal growth or careers. But that only removes part of the argument for having children late. As our world continues to grow more complex, we'll also need more education to understand and manage our daily lives. From a psychological and economic standpoint, our future crop of parents may be even less ready to marry and have children during their physical prime.

It's within our power to find solutions to this problem, too. We should be able to come up with some mechanism that will let couples mature faster than they do now. We may eventually eliminate the remaining biological barriers to having children later. But this is a vision that will take many years to realize.

We may also not want to restrict future generations to a single lifestyle or marriage form. Authorities such as Margaret Mead and Jessie Bernard look forward to a future of much diversity in family life. "There will be . . . options that permit different kinds of relationships over time for different stages in life, and options that permit different lifestyles or living arrangements according to the nature of the relationships," predicts Professor Bernard. "There may be, up to about age twenty-five, options for childless liaisons; for the years of maturity, stable and at least 'temporarily permanent' marriages involving child rearing; for middle age and beyond, new forms of relationships. People will be able to tailor their relationships to their circumstances and preferences. The most characteristic aspect of marriage in the future will be precisely the array of options available to different people who want different things from their relationships with one another."

One of these options is parenthood delayed past the biological prime, and it has already become a viable family form. There are trade-offs to waiting to have children past thirty, but our technology has lowered, and most likely will continue to lower, the physical price. Let's at least recognize that when we have our children is a matter of choice and that we now have the means to decide which choice is for us.

Suggestions for Further Reading

There are countless books on pregnancy, birth, and child rearing, but very few specifically for older parents. These, I believe, are of particular interest to older couples.

PREGNANCY, CHILDBIRTH, AND FAMILY PLANNING

Apgar, Virginia, M.D., M.P.H., and Joan Beck. *Is My Baby All Right?* New York: Pocket Books, 1974. Provides a highly detailed discussion of birth defects, including those associated with parental age, and of how to combat them.

Bean, Constance. *Methods of Childbirth.* New York: Dolphin Books, 1974. A guide to current childbirth methods and childbirth education.

Bing, Elizabeth, R.P.T. *Six Practical Lessons for an Easier Childbirth.* New York: Bantam Books, 1969. Mrs. Bing's Lamaze course, especially useful for couples who can't attend childbirth classes.

Boston Women's Health Book Collective. *Our Bodies, Ourselves.* New York: Simon and Schuster, 1976. Comprehensive guide to female sexuality and health care. Features a stimulating but controversial chapter on pregnancy and a sensitive discussion of infertility and other childbearing problems.

Cherry, Sheldon H., M.D. *Understanding Pregnancy and Childbirth.* New York: Bantam Books, 1975. The basics of pregnancy and delivery, clearly and sympathetically presented. Includes an excellent chapter on the Lamaze method of prepared childbirth.

Davis, Adelle. *Let's Have Healthy Children.* New York: Signet Books, 1972. Detailed nutritional guide for expectant mothers, babies, and young children.

Guttmacher, Alan, M.D. *Pregnancy, Birth and Family Planning.* New York: Signet Books, 1973. In-depth discussion of the mechanics of pregnancy and family planning, but not very supportive of late pregnancies.

Kaufman, S. A. *New Hope for the Childless Couple: The Causes and Treatment of Infertility.* New York: Simon and Schuster, 1970. May be helpful to those with fertility problems.

McCauley, Carole Spearin. *Pregnancy after Thirty-five.* New York: E. P. Dutton, 1976. General survey of childbirth methods, with a quick look at the medical side of late pregnancy.

Whelan, Elizabeth M., M.D., Sc.D. *The Pregnancy Experience.* New York: W. W. Norton, 1978. A look at the psychological aspects of pregnancy, changing feelings about oneself and others, with suggestions for coping with depression during pregnancy.

PARENTING AND CHILD REARING

Barber, Virginia, and Merrill Maguire Skaggs. *The Mother Person.* Indianapolis and New York: The Bobbs-Merrill Company, 1975. Describes what it's like to become a parent, with a few helpful suggestions for coping with young children.

Kappelman, Murray, M.D. *Raising the Only Child.* New York: E. P. Dutton, 1975. Encouraging advice for one-child families.

Levine, James. *Who Will Raise the Children?* New York: Bantam Books, 1977. Path-breaking study of how fathers can and should become more involved in parenting.

Spock, Benjamin, M.D. *Baby and Child Care.* New York: Pocket Books, 1975. Revised and enlarged version of the postwar classic, more supportive of working mothers than earlier editions.

Whelan, Elizabeth M., M.D., Sc.D. *A Baby? Maybe: A Guide to Making the Most Fateful Decision of Your Life.* Indianapolis and New York: The Bobbs-Merrill Company, 1975. Outlines the considerations for deciding to have children.

CAREER AND FAMILY

Bernard, Jessie. *The Future of Motherhood.* New York: Penguin Books, 1975. Puts the institution of motherhood into historical and sociological perspective. Bernard's critique of current child-rearing practices is highly encouraging for working mothers.

Curtis, Jean. *Working Mothers.* Garden City, New York: Doubleday and Co., Inc., 1976. Suggestions to make combining job and family easier, based on 200 interviews.

Epstein, Cynthia. *A Woman's Place.* Berkeley and Los Angeles: University of California Press, 1971. Pioneering study of the obstacles to combining motherhood and career.

Illustrated Woman's Almanac, eds. Kathryn Paulsen and Ryan A. Kuhn. Philadelphia and New York: J. B. Lippincott, 1976. Among its twelve "how to" handbooks are sections on motherhood, work, setting up a business, and financial and legal advice. A most useful compendium for women.